THE MELENDY QUARTET

The Saturdays
The Four-Story Mistake
Then There Were Five
Spiderweb for Two: A Melendy Maze

Then There Were Five

Written and Illustrated by

Elizabeth Enright

A MELENDY QUARTET BOOK

Henry Holt and Company

SQUARE FISH

For Two Roberts

An Imprint of Macmillan

Library of Congress Cataloging-in-Publication Data
Enright, Elizabeth, 1909–1968.
Then there were five: a Melendy book / written and illustrated by Elizabeth Enright.
p. cm.
Sequel to: The Four-Story Mistake. Sequel: Spiderweb for two.
Originaly published: [New York] : Holt, Rinehart and Winston, 1944.
Summary: A summer that promises to be eventful turns into something extra special when the four Melendy children become friends with the orphaned Mark Herron.
[1. Brothers and sisters—Fiction. 2. Orphans—Fiction. 3. Country life—Fiction.] I. Title.
PZ7.E724 Te2002 [Fic]—dc21 2001051898
ISBN-13: 978-0-312-37600-0 / ISBN-10: 0-312-37600-6

First published in hardcover in 1944 by Holt, Rinehart and Winston.
Reissued in hardcover in 2002 by Henry Holt and Company, with an introduction by Elizabeth Enright from *The Melendy Family*, copyright © 1947.
First Square Fish Edition: February 2008
Square Fish logo designed by Filomena Tuosto
10 9 8 7 6 5 4 3 2 1
www.squarefishbooks.com

Contents

Introduction

Quite often I receive letters from children asking to know if the Melendys are "real." Are Mona, Rush, Randy, and Oliver really alive? they ask. Or were they ever? Was there once a real Cuffy, or a real Isaac? Or a house called the Four-Story Mistake?

The answers to these questions are mixed. It must be admitted that such a family, made of flesh and blood, whom one could touch, talk to, argue with, and invite to parties, does not actually exist. Yet in other ways, as I shall try to show, each of these people is at least partly real.

Once, when I was a child, I heard of a family named Melendy. I do not know how many children were in this family, or what kind of people they were; but for some reason I liked their name and stored it away in my mind to borrow for the Four-Story children at a much later date. So they began, at least, with a real name.

As I went along I borrowed other things: qualities, habits, remarks, events. I borrowed them from my children, from my own childhood, even from the dogs we have had; and from the conversations and recollections of many of our friends and relatives.

Mona and Randy, for instance, are partly made of things I remember about myself as a child (only the better things, of course), and things that I wish I had been, and that I would like to have had in daughters of my own. In Mona I also recognize my dearest cousin, as well as my roommate in boarding school who was going to be an actress, and who was frequently discovered acting the part of Joan of Arc in front of the bathroom mirror.

In Randy I recognize two of my long-ago best friends, as well as two of my long-ago best wishes: to be a dancer and to be an artist.

In Oliver I have borrowed liberally from the things I know and remember about my sons, and from many other little boys besides. Large patches of him are invented, of course, which is also true of the others. I never knew of a boy of six, for instance, who got away with an adventure like Oliver's Saturday excursion, but on the other hand I have been intimately concerned with a boy who collected moths just as ardently as Oliver did. The whole family was involved in this hobby of his: all of us went through the grief of caterpillars lost, strayed or perished; through the inconvenience of cocoons hung up in the wrong places, and the foragings by flashlight for special leaves to feed ravenous larvae while the forgetful collector slept in deepest calm.

Reminders of my sons' characters also occur in that of Rush, though not so often as in the case of Oliver. In Rush I trace memories of other boys I knew: one who played the piano marvelously well, and one who was a curly-haired rascal with a large vocabulary and a propensity for getting into, and neatly out of, trouble.

Cuffy is someone I knew when I was five years old, and someone else I knew when I was twelve. One of them was rather cross, the other very gentle. Both of them were fat people, elderly, and, in their different ways, knew how to love children so that they felt comfortable and cozy.

Father is composed of several fathers of my acquaintance, all of them kind and hard-working and deeply interested in their children.

As for Isaac, except for the fact that he is a male and not pure-blooded, he is exactly like our own fat freckled cocker spaniel who was gloriously won in a raffle by the father in our family.

The house which is called the Four-Story Mistake is made out of several queer old interesting houses that I have seen and is set in the kind of country which I have enjoyed the most: country with plenty of woods, hills, streams, and valleys.

Wishing has played a large part in these stories too, as

you can see. The Melendys have and do all the things I would have liked to have and do as a child. There are plenty of them, for one thing, and I was an only child. They live in the country all year round, for another, and I lived in the city for most of it. They discovered a secret room, built a tree house, found a diamond, escaped from dangers, effected rescues, gave elaborate theatrical performances at the drop of a hat, got lost, and did many other striking things, all of which I would have liked to do.

So the Melendys, you see, are a mixture. They are made out of wishes and memory and fancy. This I am sure is what all the characters in books are made of; yet while I was writing about these children they often seemed to me like people that I knew; and when you are reading the stories of their trials and adventures I hope that you, too, will sometimes feel that they are "real."

—Elizabeth Enright, 1947

Then There Were Five

CHAPTER I

All Summer Long

What a noise there was that day! It sounded like a pack of young sea lions.

But it was really only the Melendy children. They were building a dam.

Rush had thought of it. He had thought of it in the middle of the night in a dream, and this morning at breakfast he had told them about it.

"Listen, kids," he'd said. "I've been thinking for a long time that we needed a bigger swimming place. The one we've got now is too little; when we're all in it together the congestion is fierce. And it's too shallow. Every time

I dive off the bank I'm scared I'll come up with concussion of the brain."

"Well, what are you planning to do?" inquired Mona with a tinge of sarcasm. "Widen the brook, or deepen it, or something?"

"Exactly, my dear Watson," replied Rush with a flourish of toast. "I propose to build a dam at the foot of the bathing pool where the waterfall begins."

Oliver and Randy greeted the idea with enthusiasm. Anything, work or play, that involved plenty of water and mud was agreeable to them. And even Mona could see that the idea had its points.

So there they were, hard at it, digging up rocks, hauling logs, and building them into a sort of walk across the brook. Everybody had ideas as to how the dam should be constructed. The air rang, quivered, with commands, directions, opinions, and arguments. Frequent arguments; and all carried on at an earsplitting pitch in competition with the noisy little waterfall.

The two dogs, Isaac and John Doe, added to the general pandemonium by running to and fro on the bank and barking. They always barked when voices were raised.

It was strange how the character of each Melendy was shown in his work.

Take Rush, for instance. He was fourteen and strong for his age. His bare ribs, like an Indian brave's, were striped with mud where he had slapped furiously at mosquitoes. He worked violently and fast: lugged the biggest rocks, lifted the heaviest loads, grunted, struggled, perspired, and from time to time was forced to give in and rest, from sheer exhaustion.

Mona was the eldest. She was very pretty and quite old: past fifteen. Her job was to stuff the chinks between the stones with dead leaves, wads of moss and grass, anything to keep the water from pouring through. This she did efficiently and quickly, pausing now and then to look at her own dark reflection in the pool or to wash the mud from her fastidious fingers. She was certainly the only one who bothered to do that.

Oliver, who was seven and three-quarters, worked like a little engine on a track. Back and forth he went, over and over, never getting tired because he never handled more than he could manage.

Randy, twelve, was the one who slipped and stumbled oftenest. Strange that Randy, who drew so well and danced like a fairy, should be so clumsy at manual labor. Already she had a swollen toe and a bruised thumb. Heaven knows what she would have before the day was over! Yet in spite of the punishment she took Randy enjoyed this engineering and her dark curls shook and quivered in the ardor of her exertion.

"It's sprung another leak over here, Rush," called Oliver, imparting the bad news with an air of gratified importance.

"My gosh, *again*?" Rush splashed over to the spot. "This job is tougher than I thought it would be. How do the beavers do it?"

"Well, for one thing, they have tails as well as hands to work with," said Mona, scooping up dead leaves.

"Yes, and teeth," agreed Rush. "Every beaver I ever saw had teeth like a Japanese general's."

"Don't be discouraged, Rush," said Randy piously. "Think of Boulder Dam. I bet *those* men didn't get discouraged."

Rush had to laugh at that.

By noon, however, the dam looked something like a dam, and the pool was beginning to fill up. "Another couple of days—" Rush said.

"What about lunch?" inquired Oliver practically. He was feeling the justified hunger pangs of a day laborer.

"Oh, lunch!" Rush was cross. "That's the trouble with life. You get to work on an idea, or a piece of music, or—or a dam, or something. All concentrated and working right, and then suddenly at an arbitrary time you have to stop and eat food. Chew and swallow, chew and swallow, three times a day! It's a silly habit."

"Trouble with you is you're hungry," said Mona tranquilly. "And you're cross because you know you'll have to wash off all that mud before Cuffy lets you in the house."

"What's an arbitrary time?" asked Oliver.

"Lunchtime, I guess he means," Randy told him. "Oh, look, here comes Cuffy! And I think—yes, how swell—she *has* got our lunch with her!"

Good old Cuffy! They watched her coming toward

them, white and fat and round, like a pigeon on the lawn. She had a basket and a thermos bottle. When they flung themselves upon her in gratitude and greed she brushed them aside.

"Go on with you!" she scolded, pretending to be annoyed. "I just wanted to keep your muddy tracks out of the house."

But the Melendys knew that that was only partly true. Cuffy believed in a little pleasant spoiling blended with discipline. She had been taking care of them so long that in many ways they felt as if she were their mother, whom they had lost a long time before. Or more like a very special grandmother, perhaps, since she was white-haired and roly-poly.

"Cuffy, you come and eat with us," said Oliver, pushing his dirty paw into her clean, pink one.

"No, no, my lamb. I'm going to mop myself into a corner of the kitchen and have a cup of tea. And don't one of you *dare* come in until it's dry!"

The children sat on the grass with their bare muddy legs stretched out before them in the sunshine. The brook sang and tinkled in the shade. Across the lawn, all smothered in vines and sheltered by Norway spruce trees, stood their house; the strange house that they lived in and that they loved. It was a square old building, with quantities of ornamental iron trimming, a mansard roof, and a fancy little cupola, like a frosted cake, perched on top of it. The Four-Story Mistake, the house was called, because years ago when it was built the architect had made a mistake and left off a story. The Melendys had only moved into it in the fall, but they did not like to believe that they had ever lived anywhere else. There were still surprises that it could give them, though. Now that June was here the old ragged-looking vine over the kitchen door had suddenly become a cascade of little yellow roses that smelled like tea. The grass in the orchard was full of tiny wild strawberries, hot from the sun and sweet as honey, and in the spruce tree outside Rush's window an oriole had built its nest, a silver purse full of gold.

"All summer!" said Rush, with his mouth full. "Think of it. All summer long."

"All summer what?" Mona wanted to know.

"Just all summer," Rush said happily. "I mean this is only the beginning of it. Dams and swimming and the garden and picnics and hot days and all. Oh, boy."

"Sometimes it will rain. And sometimes we'll get stomachaches. And sometimes Cuffy will be cross," said Oliver realistically.

Rush laughed. "A pessimist at seven."

"Eight," said Oliver. "Almost. I get a birthday pretty soon. What's a pessimist?"

By the end of the afternoon the dam was finished. Randy looked at it in consternation.

"But now there's no waterfall!" she cried. "I didn't think about there being no waterfall. Just that little trickle. I miss the noise."

"Silly, that's the point," said Rush. "Cut off the waterfall and up comes the pool. When it gets high enough it'll slop over the top again. And look how swell it will be for swimming."

"Well, I guess so." Randy was doubtful.

"Will it be full enough tomorrow when we wake up?" said Oliver.

"Nope. Not tomorrow, and not the day after. But maybe the day after *that*."

More than two days. Oliver felt it might as well have been a month. He had supposed the pool would fill right up like a bathtub. He was disgusted.

They had worked hard. The dam was twice as thick as necessary, and it zigzagged like the Great Wall of China; but it was strong and well-constructed. They were pleased with their work, even though it was now finished and they were muddy and would have to take baths. To her collection of wounds Randy had added a gash on the shin.

"How did you get away without knocking one of your teeth out?" Rush said. "Overlook it?"

"Randy puts her whole soul into her work," Mona defended her sister.

"Okay. Just so long as she doesn't put her front teeth into it, too."

"He jests at scars that never felt a wound," remarked Mona gloomily. She was fond of quoting Shakespeare. But in the next moment she ruined the effect by breaking into a gallop and shouting over her shoulder at Randy, "First dibs on the bathtub!"

She almost crashed into Willy Sloper coming around the corner of the house. He had changed from his customary overalls to his blue serge suit. "How many of you folks want to drive to the train with me to meet your papa?"

All of them did, even the dogs. They left no doubt in Willy's mind about that.

"Well, hurry up 'n' git tidy then. I can't take you to town all muddy like that. I just cleaned off the carriage this afternoon."

He certainly had. Half an hour later when they were all in the surrey the odor of cleaning fluid was almost asphyxiating.

"Nobody light a match," cautioned Rush unnecessarily. "We'd explode like a block buster."

"If you hang your head over the side it's not so bad," said Randy, who was less in than out of the carriage. As for Mona, she was holding a heavily perfumed handkerchief up to her nose and rolling her eyes above it like one of those fainting heroines in an old-fashioned novel.

Oliver was sitting beside Willy in the front seat. "I don't see why you mind it," he said stolidly to the three in the back. "I think it's a nice smell." He gave a loud relishing sniff to prove it. "M-m-m. Good."

Willy smiled at him. "You're my pal, aintcha? Anyways it'll wear off in time."

"Well, it looks just lovely, Willy, anyway," Mona said. "It never looked so nice."

Willy was pleased. "Ought to. Besides cleanin' them seats I brushed it all out with the whisk broom. And I took and put Vaseline on the dashboard to kind of limber it up, and then I shined it up good with black shoe polish—"

"Ah, that explains the peculiar bouquet," remarked Rush, breathing deeply. "I thought it couldn't be just only cleaning fluid."

"—And notice the fringe?" continued Willy, ignoring him.

"Why, it's all untangled."

"Combed it," said Willy. "Combed it right out, just as tender as if it was a baby's hair."

"Lorna Doone looks nice, too," Randy said. The dappled horse had roses stuck in the bridle above her ears. From the front, with her long eyelashes and comblike blinkers she resembled a very homely Spanish señorita, but from the side and back the effect was both spirited and dressy.

"Father will be pleased," Mona said happily. For of course all this grandeur was for Father. He had not been home for two whole weeks.

"Maybe he can stay all the time now, like he used to," Randy said hopefully. "Maybe he won't even have to go and lecture anymore."

"Fat chance," said Rush, "with the war going on.

Probably he'll have to be away even more."

And that is exactly what was to happen. After the joyful confusion of arrival, the hugs, the shouts, the bits of news that couldn't wait; after Father had had his hat knocked off and brushed and put on again, and his briefcase and suitcase wrested away from him; after he had shaken hands with Willy, and admired the surrey, and patted Lorna Doone and given her a lump of train sugar ("Don't let Washington hear about this," said Father); after they were all packed in the surrey and Braxton lay far behind, and the green country meadows lapped the road edge in green waves, Randy asked the question.

"Will you have to go away anymore, Father? Say you won't! Say you'll stay here now with us all the time!"

Father pulled one of Randy's curls.

"I wish I could."

"Well, why can't you? You used to."

"Used-to doesn't mean anything anymore, Randy. The used-to world is all cut away from us now; floating away in the distance like a balloon or a bubble. It isn't real any longer. Perhaps it's a good thing that it's gone. I hope so."

Oliver, like a small retriever, nosed out the fact that lay beneath these words.

"You mean you're going to have to go away again?"

Father nodded. "I'm going to have to go away again. And stay longer."

Randy sat up. "Are you going to be a soldier?"

Father laughed. "Unfortunately I'm too old. And too

decidedly a father. I have to keep busy getting worms for my young."

"Why can't you dig them up at home?" pleaded Randy.

"Because I'm going to dig them up in Washington in a large government-owned bird sanctuary."

"Gosh!" Rush said. "Have you got a government job?"

"That's right. A fascinating one, too."

"Doing what?"

"Secret," said Father complacently. "So secret that I even have to guard against talking to myself."

"How often can you come home?" said Mona.

"A weekend now and then. And perhaps two weeks in August."

This was gloomy news. They contemplated it resentfully. "You might just as well be a soldier after all," sighed Randy.

"Yes, and that way you'd at least get a medal," said Oliver.

But it was so wonderful to have him with them even for a short time; and the day was so perfect, the country so downy with the new summer, that they couldn't be sad for long.

As they turned in at the gate of the Four-Story Mistake, Rush said, "We have a surprise for you. We made it today."

"Let's save it for last though," said Mona.

And as always when Father returned they led him about the place on a tour of inspection.

First they went to the vegetable garden.

"I killed those," said Oliver with bloodthirsty satisfaction, pointing to a huge pile of dead weeds.

"The best type of killing one can do," Father approved.

He was made to look at the onions and remark upon how tall they'd grown; and the carrots, the beets, the tomato plants.

"Look at the peas," said Mona. "They really have little beginnings of pods on them. And the lettuce has stopped looking like a ruffle. You can tell it's lettuce now."

"And see the corn," Oliver pointed out. "I don't pull it up for quack grass anymore; and the radishes are getting too big already. But something keeps eating the cabbages."

"I hope it eats them all before they get a chance to ripen," observed Rush darkly. "And I've already spoken to a couple of caterpillars I know about the broccoli."

"Sulphur and iron," said Mona in exactly Cuffy's voice. "Growing children need lots of sulphur and iron."

"I'd rather eat them in their mineral state," Rush said.

Then they took Father to look at the raspberry bushes (another summer surprise produced by the Four-Story Mistake), and then to see the rose moss, but it was all closed up, and the delphiniums, just coming out, that Mona had planted.

"I love delphinium buds," Randy said. "They're exactly like big blue tadpoles."

The Canterbury bells were just beginning too, but the

columbine and bleeding hearts were nearly over. Soon there would be hollyhocks and phlox.

They took him to see Persephone, the goat, and her new kid; and Willy's white chickens that he kept behind the stable, and last of all they took him down to see the dam.

Father was overwhelmed.

"What a piece of engineering," he cried. "So strong and so—so big. It would take the Johnstown flood to break it open. How long did it take you to do it?"

"Just all day," Rush told him modestly. "But of course there were four of us working on it."

"When I come up next time I'll enjoy swimming in it. Before this the water in the deepest part came only to my collarbone."

As they stood contemplating it, Father silent in admiration and the rest of them silent in the pride of creation, there was a piercing blast from the front door of the house. It was Cuffy blowing the police whistle, and it meant that supper was ready.

Randy danced across the lawn ahead of Father. "Look, I can walk on my toes. Almost! And in sneakers, too. When can I have a pair of real toe shoes, do you think?"

Mona's arm was linked through Father's and Oliver was hanging onto his other hand. Rush walked beside them and everybody was talking at once. Isaac and John Doe circled around them madly barking and scuffling; showing Father what big, serious dogs they had become. A delicious fragrance of food floated from the kitchen windows.

"Wait till you hear my new piece," Rush was saying. "It's a Schumann Novelette and, boy, is it tough!"

Mona said, "I know the whole of *Macbeth* by heart now. All the parts. I'll do it all for you after supper if you like."

Oliver said, "Did you see the President in Washington, Father? Did you get to shake his hand? Did you talk to him?"

And Randy, circling among the circling dogs, flitting and soaring like a moth, kept calling the same question:

"Do you think I could have some toe shoes pretty soon, Father? Real toe shoes, pink satin ones, with satin ribbons? Do you think I can, Father? Do you? Honestly, do you?"

Cuffy had all Father's favorite things for supper, beginning with leek and potato soup and building up to a grand finale of strawberry pie.

Afterward they went out again. The birds were carrying on all over the place, and a little crowd of swallows flew high overhead chattering like children out of school. The grass and leaves smelled of evening and there was a coolness around one's ankles. Rush wanted to start a game of Prisoner's Base, but Father said no, that he couldn't run because he was pie-bound.

He sat on the front steps smoking his pipe. Already the pale, strained city look was beginning to leave him.

Rush and Mona and Randy sat beside him, but Oliver walked about by himself, watching the dusk creep out of the woods. Everything was changing. The two iron deer now looked like proud, pausing, live animals, and when he went into the summer house it was filled with such a mysterious green twilight that he felt very lonely suddenly, and walked out slowly, his neck prickling, and everything about him hurrying except his feet. He would not let them hurry, nor would he let his head turn to look back.

High in the sky the first star came out like a flower. Still walking, Oliver looked up and spoke to it.

> *"Star light, star bright,*
> *First star I see tonight*
> *Wish I may, wish I might*
> *Have the wish I wish tonight."*

Oliver wished that someone would give him a little helicopter for his birthday. Then he walked the rest of the way with his head bowed, staring at his shoes. If he glimpsed the star again his wish would be lost.

Father was beginning to yawn.

"I thi—oh, I think I'd be—oh, I'd better go—oh—oh—to bed."

"Fresh air. Can't take it, eh?" said Rush.

"No. Too strong for me. You should see how brilliant

and alert I am on carbon monoxide fumes and ci—oh—oh—ah—cigar smoke."

"He's so tired," Mona said when he had gone. "It's awful he has to work so hard."

"Digging worms for us," said Rush. "And trying to do his bit besides. I wish I could do something to help. I wish I could be of some use."

"Oh, Rush, you are a help," Randy cried. "You earn every bit of your own spending money giving those piano lessons. Mona earns all of her own living acting on the radio twice a week in *The Penfold People*. What do I do? I don't do anything, that's what. It seems as if I'm the only really dependent one in the place besides the dogs. And Oliver, of course, but he's so young he couldn't—"

"I could take ticks off dogs for people," said Oliver sternly. "I'm good at it. I could go around to people's houses with a bottle and some tweezers, and maybe they'd pay me a penny apiece—"

"That's not what I mean exactly," interrupted Rush. "Not just money. If we keep somebody from going to war by being dependents, then it seems as if we ought to do extra things about helping generally."

"Would they take any people as young as me in the army?" cried Oliver, his eyes shining. "I could clean out the insides of cannons, for instance. I'm a good size for it."

"Oh, *no*, Oliver. Don't be silly. The best thing you can do is keep after the weeds in the vegetable garden."

Weeds. Oliver's face clouded. He knew plenty about

them by now. There was one called purslane, with a lot of fat, pink tentacles, that grew up overnight in countless numbers. There was quack grass, coarse and hardy, its roots stretching under the earth in endless nets. There were yellow dock, and lamb's-quarters, and velvetleaf . . . such stubborn boring little enemies. Oliver would have liked to be up in the sky shooting down Zeros, instead of down on the earth pulling up weeds.

"Mona knits and she's done first aid, of course . . . Not that she remembers any of it."

"Artificial respiration!" cried Mona. "I remember artificial respiration perfectly. Get down on your stomach and I'll show—"

"No, thank you. I won't let you demonstrate it on me until you remember what kind of bandage to put on cracked ribs."

"I think you're mean. I was the best in the class at artificial respiration. Miss McCarthy said so."

"All right. You can be the one who resuscitates drowning persons from now on. But since the opportunities for this type of work are few and far between, and since you are off the radio for the summer, I suggest you do something else. Help Cuffy, for instance. People are supposed to can a lot of food, aren't they?"

That sounded pleasant and rather simple, as well as comfortably far in the future, since practically nothing was ripe yet. Mona agreed graciously.

"Randy and I will go out and collect scrap. We'll have

a scrap drive. And I mean a *drive*. We'll hitch Lorna Doone to the surrey, and we'll go to all the backwoods farms up in the hills and see what we can dig up. I think it's a swell idea. We'll drive the buggy, see, and on the back of it we'll have a sign saying Scrap Drive. Get it?"

"Too subtle for me," said Mona sarcastically. But Randy and Oliver thought it was a brilliant idea.

"It sounds nicer than weeds," Oliver commented wistfully, and Randy promised to let him take her place part of the time.

"We'll start Monday after Father's gone," Rush decided. "I'm bushed. All that work on the dam, I guess. And, Oliver, you should have been in bed ages ago. Cuffy only let you stay up because Father was here. Scram!"

"Ooh, how my muscles hurt," groaned Mona, getting up from the steps. "All kinds of little ones that I didn't know I had. It even hurts me to sigh."

Tired as they were, however, the Melendys didn't fall asleep immediately that night. Their usual lullaby had been removed for the time being, and they missed it. Instead of the soft, rushing, varying harmonies of the waterfall there was the dark silence of a country night. This silence was woven of many small sounds: of soft, long owl calls, of tree frogs' voices, of invisible wings fluttering past a window, and above all the delicate, ceaseless breathing of the woods.

CHAPTER II

A Talent for Trash

On Monday afternoon Rush harnessed Lorna Doone to the surrey. Cuffy gave them an old bedspread to protect the back seat, and he and Randy sat up in front. It was a wonderful hot afternoon. There had been no rain for a long time, and the dust lifted in clouds from the road. Beside the road the draperies of clematis and wild honeysuckle, the ditch armies of milkweed and bouncing bet, were white with an ashy powdering of dust. Beyond them rose the woods, full of new leaves; full of green light and shade. The surrey smelled of dust and hot leather and

Lorna Doone; but from the woods came faintly a cool, mysterious scent of moss and ancient earth.

Sunlight glittered on the whip.

"Oh, Rush, isn't it fun," cried Randy. "Just you and me off exploring like this."

"On a mission for our government, you mean," Rush said rather stiffly, but a second later he turned and grinned at her. "It's nifty," he agreed.

"Let's try this one," suggested Randy. A road turned off to the right. Beside it stood a mailbox on a post. The post was planted firmly in a large milk can filled with earth, and around its foot a frill of timothy and a daisy had also planted themselves in a sort of little garden.

"Addison," Randy read on the mailbox. "That sounds like a good sensible name."

He pulled a rein and Lorna Doone turned in. She walked slowly, for the road wound upward. Her hindquarters moved up and down, up and down, like two rocking, shining hills, and her tail switched at the flies.

"What do you think they'll be like, the Addisons?" Rush wondered lazily. "Or maybe it's only one, a single Addison. I seem to see them as tall people with square jaws. Kind of serious and industrious and not laughing much."

"Oh, *I* don't," Randy said. "I think they're two old, jolly people. Fat, you know, with morning-glories, and baby chickens, and calves, and maybe some cookies—"

"A confused description, but I get the general picture,"

Rush said. "Whichever one is wrong has to wash the supper dishes tonight."

The road sloped gently upward. It was flanked on either side by Austrian pines whose branches were longer on one side than the other as if the wind blew always from the same quarter. Beyond the trees the pastures sloped up on the right and down on the left. Small Swiss cattle dotted the hillside. They were cream-colored darkening to mushroom brown.

"They're much prettier than the usual cow," Randy said. "They look more like real animals. Deer or antelope or something."

Mourning doves cooed softly everywhere and a pair of truant white hens picked their foolish way along the road.

They rounded the bend, and there, nestled in a curve of hillside, lay the farmhouse, like an egg in a nest. It was white, the way all good farmhouses should be, and it was shaded by two huge soft maple trees; two tall fountains of green leaves. Flowers grew along the fence, and not only along the fence but in unexpected, haphazard clusters in the grass. In one place there were frail pink poppies dropping their petals in the slightest breeze; in another there was a steeple of hollyhocks. There was a swing hanging from one of the maples, and near the house in a little pen stood a baby with a fluff of yellow hair.

The house was smothered in vines and shrubs; and its breath came out of it sweet and warm, smelling of gingerbread.

"Hello, baby," said Rush. "Folks home?"

"Ba," replied the baby, drooling.

"He's cute, Rush. He looks the way Oliver used to. His hair kind of grows sideways like his did."

"But they don't really get faces till they're around four years old," said Rush, losing interest.

They knocked on the screen door and looked in. They could see a big black coal stove and not much else. There was a soft padding of bare feet. A little girl about ten years old looked out at them. She wore a faded blue calico dress, her cheeks and nose were pink with sunburn, and her blond hair fell straight to her shoulders.

"Hello," she said. "Who are you?"

"We're the Melendys," Rush told her. "At least we're some of them. We came to see if you people had any scrap for the government."

"Scrap? You mean used metal for the soldiers?"

"That's it."

"Well, wait; I'll ask Mom. You can come in." She held the door open. "I'm baking some gingerbread."

"You are?" Randy was impressed. "Do you know *how?*"

"Yes. It's in the oven now. You can smell it. Smell it?"

"M-m-m." Rush lifted his nose rapturously, and looked as if he were going to bay like a wolfhound.

"Well, you folks sit down. I'll get Mom."

The girl went out of the room. They heard her bare feet flipping upstairs.

"Nice," Randy said, looking around the big country

kitchen with its table already set for supper; its red linoleum floor; its green vine-covered windows like windows under a waterfall.

"Swell," agreed Rush. They sat there not saying anything else; shy of their own voices in this stranger's house.

The bare footsteps came down the stairs again, followed by grown-up ones in shoes. A tall lady in a lavender dress followed the little girl into the kitchen.

"Hello," said the lady. "So you're the Melendys. We are the Addisons. I am Mrs. Addison and this is my daughter Daphne."

"And I'm Rush and this is my sister Miranda."

"Randy!" corrected Randy indignantly.

"I understand you've come to collect scrap, and I'm very glad to see you because we have lots of it. I hope you have some way of carrying it?"

"Our carriage," said Rush elegantly.

"Daphne, run get Dave. He can round up the stuff. Or better still take Rush and Randy with you, and show them our barn." She turned to them. "Dave's been helping his father get the hay in before it rains again."

They went out the door behind Daphne. She had almost stopped being shy, and as they passed the baby she said, "That's my brother Alexander. He's getting another tooth. That's why he looks at you folks like that."

The baby was scowling at them.

"Alexander Addison," said Rush. "With that name he's going to have to amount to something. Maybe he'll grow up to be a famous inventor. Or—or a news commentator."

"Alexander Addison," repeated Randy. "He sounds like somebody who ought to have signed the Declaration of Independence. Maybe he'll be a governor or an ambassador or something."

"Pop says he'll prob'ly be a champion hog caller when he grows up," Daphne said. "On account of the way he can holler when he's mad. Here's our barn."

The barn was splendid. That was the only word for it. It was huge and crimson, and its ridgepole was ornamented with lightning rods, weather vanes, dovecots, and ventilators shaped like medieval pavilions.

"Come inside," said Daphne.

What a place it was! Lofty as a cathedral; full of the gold of hay, and its golden, heady smell. High in the dusky shadows of the roof barn swallows twittered and darted. Still above, from the ridgepole came the soft stutterings of pigeons. Straw was scattered on the floor and among it stepped a rooster with a quivering comb.

"Dave!" called Daphne.

There was no answer. She called again, and a third time.

"Dav-id! We've got company! And they're right here with me!"

There was a sudden rustling and crackling. Between the empty stalls stood the hay wagon, unhitched, and filled to overflowing with its last load. A boy slid down from it suddenly.

"Dave Addison! You heard me all the time."

The boy grinned. "Sure I did, but I was taking a short nap. What they call a siesta." He turned to Rush and Randy. "Hello. I've been out in the hayfield all day and, boy, was it hot. I got bushed. What are your names? Mine's David Addison."

Rush told him and explained their mission. He liked this boy's looks. He seemed to be about twelve or thirteen, and a strong, independent person.

"Sure we've got stuff for you. Come on with me, will you, Rush, and help me carry it."

Randy and Daphne stood in the barn looking at each other. For some reason the shyness had come back again.

"Ever tried this?" cried Daphne suddenly, and she went up the ladder to the loft quick as a monkey; poised there on the edge like an aerial performer and then suddenly, breathlessly, arched into space, into the golden shafts of sunlight with their golden motes, and landed lightly, softly in the hay wagon far below.

"I have to do that too," said Randy and up the ladder she went, hardly able to find a place to put her foot the hay bulged out so richly between the rungs.

The hay in the loft was soft and smothery, full of a golden sneezy dust. She sank into it up to her knees with every step. Poised at the edge, she hesitated, drew in her breath.

"Gee whiz, Daphne. It looks about a mile away, that wagon. What if I missed it?"

"You couldn't miss it, Randy, it's big as a boxcar. Come on, jump. It's fun, honestly it is!"

Daphne's little sun-stained face was turned up to her encouragingly, pink as a strawberry. Randy couldn't be a sissy even if she broke her leg not being one.

Take care of me, God, prayed Randy silently and leaped. Oh, what joy. Right out into the air like a bird; free as a bird and as safe. Pouf—bounce! A feathery thump, and there she was lying on her face, laughing in the sweet, scratchy hay.

"Hurry up, Randy, out of the way! I'm coming!" Daphne was standing on the edge of the loft looking down like a youthful angel contemplating the earth.

"Well, wait a minute, hold your horses. Wait till I get down!" commanded Randy. She slid from the wagon, and ran for the ladder. "Hurry up, or I'll catch you," she cried halfway up. The shyness had vanished from them both.

When they came out of the barn at last, hot and red-cheeked, there were dried clover blossoms in their hair, and bits of leaf and stalk sticking to their clothes. Daphne brushed Randy off, and Randy brushed Daphne.

"What school do you go to?" asked Randy. "I never saw you over at Carthage."

"Oh, we go to the District School. Over toward Eldred it is. A little white schoolhouse with a bell like a dinner bell. We've always gone there."

"Hey, Randy, come help!" shouted Rush's voice. He was going toward the surrey with his arms full of wire coat hangers and tin cans. David was following, dragging an old bedspring.

Daphne and Randy ran to their assistance and presently the back of the surrey was heaped with a welter of scrap. Burnt-out pots and pans, flatirons, broken rakes and spades, lead soldiers and toy cars, an ancient coffee grinder, a small old-fashioned radiator, the remains of some cast-iron lawn furniture, and a doorstop in the shape of a Scotty, that Mrs. Addison hated.

There was plenty of room for more, however, and Rush and Randy climbed reluctantly into the front seat to continue their quest.

"You come again real soon now, Randy," Daphne ordered. "I'll show you how to make gingerbread."

"You come too, Rush," said Dave, and they promised eagerly.

As they drove away the scrap clattered and jingled. It was a festive, pleasant sound.

"I feel like a gypsy tin peddler," Rush said. "It would be kind of a nice life. A wagon, and a horse, and the hardware clashing together over the bumps."

"No school," said Randy.

"No haircuts and fingernails," said Rush.

"No good clothes," said Randy.

"No worry about being late or early," said Rush.

They both sighed and were still, imagining a happy, untidy, leisurely life outdoors. Sleeping under hedges. Washing in brooks and streams. Cooking stolen chicken over a campfire. Throwing the bones over your shoulder into the dark . . .

"No dishes!" Rush began to laugh. "Oh, boy, were we ever wrong about the Addisons, at least this species of Addison. It's the supper dishes for you and me tonight, my friend."

The next mailbox they came to was in a hollow not far from its house. Jasper Titus was the name printed on it.

"Jasper Titus. Quick, Ran, what does it sound like?"

"Like a tall, cross man; kind of stingy and unforgiving."

"Check. That's what it sounds like to me. And this time if we're wrong we have to mop the kitchen floor!"

The appearance of the house carried out the general idea. It was an old house, but not old enough, and it sat squarely facing the road. It was tall, with gables and a bay window, and in spite of the wooden lacework dripping from the eaves, it looked narrow and severe. There was a window in the front door set with hard blue and orange panes of glass.

The doorbell had a handle to turn instead of a button to push. They turned it and heard a distant sound like a muffled alarm clock. Nobody came. They waited and before they had screwed up the courage to ring it again they heard a voice calling from somewhere.

"Round to the *back*! Round to the *back*! That door ain't been opened in nine years."

Randy and Rush walked around the house; around the bridal wreath bushes, and the canna plants, and an old tin washtub with pansies in it. Rush looked at it covetously. "Scrap," he said. He had been collecting it so passionately that there was a mad gleam in his eye at the sight of any metal. For him the commonest tin can had come to have the luster of silver and the lure of gold.

The back of the house was a pleasant surprise. It was nice and friendly and untidy. Dishcloths lay drying on a box bush, a white duck was wandering to and fro, and three gray kittens tumbled on the grass beside an elderly dog. There was a grapevine straggling over a trellis, a bucket upside down on a post, and a clothesline with nothing on it except some clothespins like birds perched on a telegraph wire. Beyond the strip of grass as far as the barn lay a vegetable garden with bean-pole wigwams. Here and there among the vegetables were planted loud, cheerful flowers.

The back of the house seemed to have nothing to do with the front. It was as if this were its real character while the front was just dressed up to impress visitors or scare marauders.

An old man was sitting on the back steps shelling peas. He was fat and rosy-cheeked and the only thing that kept him from resembling Santa Claus was the absence of a beard. He did have a fine mustache, though, and his hair in the sunshine was blinding white. Over his blue jeans he wore a plaid apron.

"Afternoon, folks," said he comfortably. "What would be your desire?"

Rush explained, and the old man, Mr. Titus, looked thoughtful. Peas dropped into the basin with the sound of rain.

"Scrap. Let me see now. No cans. I put up all my own stuff in good glass jars. Seems like I got a harrow out back the orchard. Been decayin' there the last nine, ten years. Prob'ly all bound down to the earth with thistles and bindweed by now. I know, though! I got a stove. Yes, sir, got a old coal stove!" He put the basin aside and lumbered to his feet.

"Too fat," said he contentedly. "Too blame fat. Been years accruin' it."

He waddled toward the barn still wearing his apron which was tied in a neat bow behind. The duck, the collie, and the kittens followed too.

Mr. Titus broke off a leaf of something, sniffed it and gave it to Randy.

"Lemon verbena," he said. "I keep it for smellin' purposes."

He led them to a shed and opened the door. It was full of the kind of things that people can't help collecting when they live for a long time in one place. There was an old-fashioned sewing machine, and dozens of Mason jars, some kerosene cans, and a shelfful of oil lamps with sooty glass chimneys; there was a parrot cage, and two wheelbarrows, flowerpots, watering cans, a hose curled up like a serpent and five calendars on the wall, each for a different year and none for the present one. There was a dressmaker's form, and a workbench with a tool rack and some very old shavings lying on it in dusty curls. There were two oil paintings, one of a man, the other of a woman; they had plain, durable faces and the mole on the lady's chin was painted with loving care. Mr. Titus looked at the pictures thoughtfully.

"My grandparents," said he. "Fine folks they was, fine folks. But I felt better having 'em out here. In the parlor they kept lookin' at me hard and sayin', 'Jasper, get on with your chores!'"

He shoved aside the sewing machine and there was the stove. A sturdy, potbellied stove that had seen years of service.

"Gee that's swell, Mr. Titus," breathed Rush, the look coming into his eye.

"What about old Mrs. Gladstone?" suggested Mr. Titus, giving the dressmaker's form a good hearty spank. "She's got a lot of metal in her. A fine stout metal carcass, and that standard."

"But—you might need it sometime," said Rush staring covetously at the dressmaker's form.

Mr. Titus laughed. "Even if I was constructed along the same general lines, I'd still have a hard time wearin' size thirty-eight. No, go on, you take her."

So they took Mrs. Gladstone, and a moment later the parrot cage. Mr. Titus helped with the stove, and brought part of a clothesline to lash down the cargo in the back of the surrey.

Before they left Rush and Randy learned a lot about Mr. Titus. They learned that he was a bachelor whose only sister had kept house for him until her late marriage nine years before. Up to that time he had been a farmer, but now he rented his barn, meadows, and pastureland and lived contentedly in his own house, with his pets.

"Always was lazy, always will be," he said. "Never did like heavy chores. Just did 'em 'cause my conscience drove me. Yes, sir, drove me. And then one day it quit, just laid down quiet and gave up the struggle. Since then no more cows! No more hosses! No more blame chickens, only just enough to lay me a soft-boiled egg or two. No more hawgs! Nothin' but small-fry pets to keep me company. No more long rows to hoe! No more corn! Just grow enough garden truck so's when I want a mess of peas for supper I can pick me a mess of peas. Same with all the rest. Always did like fussin' in a kitchen, too. Like to bake. Used to be ashamed of it when I was younger. But I ain't ashamed no more. One of my marble cakes took first prize over to Braxton Fair last year. Yep. That's what I like. Pets, and fussin' in a kitchen, and goin' fishin'. And by golly that's what I do!"

He gave them each a pocketful of cookies when they left and made them promise to return. "You and me'll go fishin'," he told Rush. "I know a pool where there's an old catfish big as a watermelon been lookin' at me mean for the last twenty years. I know another place where the sheepsheads sit right up on their tails and beg to be caught!"

"Could I come too?" pleaded Randy.

"You sure can, you sure can. You come, let me know when, and I'll bake us a cake, three-layer, marshmallow whip on top, coconut cream inside. Or a pie. How'd you like a Boston cream pie that goes down your throat just as easy and docile as anything you ever et?"

He stood smiling at them, lost in blissful reverie at the thought of the pie. Two of the kittens played with his shoelaces and the third he held, letting it nip his finger gently. The duck had tucked its web feet under it and lay on the grass as if on the surface of a pool. The dog, Hambone, lay beside it, his tongue hanging out of his mouth like a little pink flag.

They waved good-bye.

"Boston cream pie!" said Randy. "Cake, three layers, marshmallow whip on top! No wonder he's so fat!"

"Happy, though," Rush said. "It wouldn't suit *me*, but I'd say there's a man whose life fits him just like a good old pair of shoes."

"What about it, Rush, shall we go home? All that talk of food has made me hungry."

"Me too. But we still have some room left. We'll stop at the next farm we see."

They were quiet. Tree shadows lay across the road. There was pink in the sunshine now, and blue in the shadow; it was getting late. The woods were very still.

"Gosh!" said Randy suddenly. "Dishes *and* mopping the floor."

"That's right. Jasper Titus has the wrong name all right."

"Look, Rush, there's another mailbox."

This mailbox was tipped sideways on its post, its door hanging open like a broken jaw. Almost obliterated, the name O. Meeker was printed on its side in crude staggering letters.

To the left a road branched off through the woods. Hardly a road at all. Just a pair of wheel tracks with a tall furry strip of weeds between.

"It looks deserted," Rush said, as Lorna Doone turned in. She walked slowly there, the weeds knocking against her knees and slipping by, whispering against the wheel spokes. The roadside was crowded with ragweed and blackberry canes all woven together with poison ivy and wild cucumber.

"It's kind of scary," Randy said and added hastily, "I like it though!"

"Scary, my eye. Probably nothing but a dead end, and where the dickens am I going to find a place to turn?"

"What do you think the Meekers will be like, Rush? If there really are some Meekers?"

"Oh, like their name, I guess. Mild and timid, and greyish."

"Yes, and with lots of children; thin and mousy."

"*This* time if we're wrong we have to *wax* the kitchen floor after we've mopped it!"

How still it was; except for the faint rattling of the scrap there was no sound. They both jumped when a crow leaped clattering and cawing from a dead branch overhead. A little farther on there was a clearing where a cow stared at them forlornly, over a barbed-wire fence.

"She looks as if she wished she could go with us," Rush said.

Still farther on they emerged from the woods entirely, and found themselves looking across a hollow toward a tumbledown farm. There was a faded farmhouse, a half-dead pine tree full of flicker holes, and a knock-kneed barn with a crooked weather vane.

"Gee," said Rush. "Shall we go ask?"

"Why, I guess so. It looks rather unfriendly though, doesn't it?"

Suddenly as they approached two dogs sprung up from nowhere. Great shaggy mongrels with burs in their coats, barking furiously and leaping like demons at Lorna Doone.

Poor horse, she was used to gentle treatment and the suddenness of the dogs startled her terribly. She sprang forward, the surrey lurched, and off she shot like a race horse.

Randy screamed.

"Slow up, Man o' War!" cried Rush, pulling on the reins. "Doggone those doggone dogs!"

The dogs were loving it. They bounded and snapped and barked their great hollow, brutal barks. Through Randy's panic-stricken mind flashed the image of a picture on the Office wall: an old steel engraving entitled

"Pursued by Siberian Wolves." That's what they're like, she thought, seeing the dogs with horror. She flung her arms around Rush, sure that if she fell out the dreadful beasts would make short work of her.

The surrey tipped drunkenly from side to side. In the back there was a hideous banging and crashing of scrap. The stove door kept opening and slamming shut, the flat-irons cavorted madly in a tin boiler, coat hangers jangled like broken harpstrings, and Mrs. Gladstone performed a sort of revolving waltz with the rake. From time to time a small object jarred loose, flew through the air: a potlid, one roller skate, or a lead soldier. Lorna Doone's hoofs pounded, her mane whipped the air; briers snapped against the wheels and the dogs barked.

"Whoa!" Rush kept shouting. "For the love of Pete, will you please WHOA!"

"But the dogs," wailed Randy. "If she stops, the *dogs*!"

"King! Blackie!" bellowed a terrible voice, suddenly. "Quit it! Shut up!"

Randy had a vision of a man in dirty blue, his face rough with whiskers and his mouth wide open in anger. As if by magic the dogs fell away, and in a moment or two Lorna Doone gave up her mad flight and stood trembling before the knock-kneed barn. A big brown hog looked out of the pen and rumbled at them. There was a terrible, stifling smell of pigs.

"What the devil are you doin' on my place?" demanded

the man. He came striding up to them, a pitchfork in his hand and chaff sticking to his wet arms.

Rush was on the ground standing beside poor Lorna and stroking her quivering neck, and Randy was there, too, though she did not remember having got down from the surrey.

"Why-uh. We came to find out if you had any scrap to give to the government," said Rush, and after a moment added, "sir."

"Scrap?" said the man, and spat sideways without noticing.

"Yes. You know. Old metal. Cans, used wire, stove lids, any old thing. They need it for the soldiers," Rush explained.

"Old bicycles," added Randy, to her own surprise and disgust. She was blushing. Old bicycles, for heaven's sake!

"Listen, you," said the man. He came closer, and they stepped back involuntarily. He looked as if he wanted to hit them. "See that gully over there? Erosion they call that. All et away by wind and water. Have to keep it filled up or it'll get bigger. *That's* where my scrap goes! Old bed springs, plows that's rusted, baling wire. And that, by heck, is where it's goina stay. Now get out of here. Go on, beat it! And don't come back or I'll sick the dogs on you for sure!"

"You're not very patriotic, sir," said Rush. But he didn't

say it until he was back in the surrey and had Lorna Doone turned around in the right direction.

"Patriotic, my foot," said the man and spat sideways again. "I gotta live, don't I?" He seemed overtaken by a wave of fury and brandished his pitchfork at them suddenly. "Get out! Scram! Beat it!"

They couldn't make Lorna Doone hurry. She walked slowly and deliberately as suits a woman who has just had a fright.

"What an awful man!" said Randy. "I hate him!"

"A heel," agreed Rush. "I hope he hasn't any kids."

"Oh, he *couldn't* have." Randy was horrified. "He couldn't have, and be so mean."

But at the next bend in the road they met a hay wagon bulging with hay like a shaggy behemoth. It was drawn by a lean team of horses and driven by a boy of about thirteen. Rush pulled over to the side of the road. The hay wagon stopped, and the boy looked at them steadily, without smiling. He wore faded blue overalls and no shirt; you could see his ribs under his skin. His hair was sunbleached, almost white.

"Hello," said Randy. It came out in a sort of a croak; she couldn't tell whether he was going to be fierce or friendly, but risked the greeting anyhow.

"H'lo," said the boy, and to her astonishment and gratification smiled a shy, radiant smile.

"Your father's just chased us off your place," Rush said, as Lorna Doone lowered her head to the roadside weeds.

"We wondered if he had any scrap for us, but he didn't seem to feel like giving any."

"Aw, he's mean as a rattlesnake," said the boy carelessly, and seeing the shocked faces before him, added, "He's not my father. He's m' second cousin. Took me to live with him when I was orphaned."

"That seems rather kind," observed Randy, and could have kicked herself for the goody-goody way it sounded.

"Not of *him*. No, sir. It was his wife made him do it. And even then the only reason he gave in was that he figured I'd be able to work and he wouldn't have to pay me anything."

"She sounds all right, though."

"She was swell."

"Isn't she still?" asked Randy, and this time Rush kicked her himself.

"She died. Two years ago in July."

"Oh," Randy's face was hot. It was very quiet. Lorna Doone's industrious jaws could be heard chewing, a mellow, businesslike, contented sound.

"You folks say you was collecting scrap?"

"That's right."

"Well, listen. I have an old express wagon, kind of rusty now, and a tricycle that *she* gave me when I was a kid. You want 'em?"

Oh, people are wonderful, thought Randy. They are so kind to each other. All memory of the horrible man had left her mind for the moment.

"You bet we do," Rush was saying. "Just what we need. Shall we come back with you?"

"No, no!" the boy was emphatic. "He'd go for you sure—" He was quiet, and for an instant his clear eyes seemed to be looking at something in his own thoughts; something he did not like.

"I tell you what!" he said, brightening. "You folks tell me where you live, and I'll get 'em to you some way. First chance I can."

"I'm Rush Melendy, and she's Randy. We live at the Four-Story Mistake. Do you know where it is?"

"I've never been there but I've heard of it. It's got a little thing like a cabin on the roof, hasn't it? I'd sure like to see it."

"Well, come. Soon as you can. We'll show you around. What's your name, anyway?"

"Mark Herron. I'd like to come." The cloud came over his face again for a moment, and then he looked up, smiling his bright, shy smile. "Oren goes to town Wednesdays—"

"Oren?"

"Oren Meeker, that's him." The boy wagged his head sideways in the direction of the farm. "He goes to town Wednesdays. Market day. You could come over— Listen, I know a place where there's good hunting for arrowheads. I found lots there. And there's a cave back in the woods that's secret. Nobody knows about it but me. And I know where there's a bee tree, and a cliff full of cliff swallows; and a marble quarry, an old one 'bout three miles back, full of water, now, and deep. We could swim there. We could have fun. Would you come some Wednesday? Could you? Both of you?"

Dazzled by the riches he offered, Rush said, "You bet!" But Randy hesitated.

"What about *him*—Mr. Meeker? Won't you catch it if he finds out?"

"Maybe he won't find out. And if he does—I don't care!"

"We'll come," Randy promised. "We will come."

They said good-bye and drove back to the side road.

"He's a nice guy," Rush said.

"And lonesome," added Randy. Thinking of him now she realized that she had never seen anyone so lonely in her life.

They were tired and hungry, suddenly. So was Lorna Doone, her head drooped and the swish of her tail was languid. The woods were deep and full of secrets; they seemed to grow taller in the evening. From the ditches came the accentuated fragrance of bouncing bet.

"Gee whiz!" said Randy, suddenly sitting up straight. "Gosh. The dishes *and* the mopping *and* the waxing. Gee whiz."

Rush laughed. "I know. As character guessers we're not so hot. But as junk collectors," he looked over his shoulder at the booty in the back seat. "As junk collectors we rate a Navy E."

CHAPTER III

Shakespeare and the *Hot* Spell

The Four-Story Mistake slumbered in a cave of green. The Norway spruces stood beside it full of black shadows; and close to them grew the oaks, the elms, the sycamores. Down by the brook there were weeping willows and maples. The lawns, thanks to the industrious labors of Willy and the loudly expostulating ones of Rush, were as green as an emerald, and as soft as the nose of a pony. Beyond the lawns the woods began; flooding the valley and the hills in wave upon wave, in boundless tides of green.

Mona fanned herself with a handkerchief as she walked across the grass. It had been terribly hot for the past ten days. No wind to start a murmuring in all those green fathoms. At night the curtains hung motionless beside the open windows. Out of doors even the stars looked hot, like embers in the sky, and down under the willows the slow-roaming lights of fireflies came and vanished, came and vanished, all night long. As usual in such weather people did nothing but ask each other the same old useless question with variations, "Isn't it hot? My, isn't it hot? Boy, is it ever hot? Goodness, aren't you just *roasting*?"

People say the silliest things, thought Mona scornfully, as she started up the wooded hill. I bet Shakespeare never asked anybody if it wasn't hot. She tried to remember if he had ever written anything about hot weather, and was pleased to remember one quotation immediately:

"*Fear no more the heat o' the sun . . .*"

I wonder how many girls my age could quote Shakespeare on suitable occasions the way I can, thought Mona, and instantly stubbed her toe on a rock. Probably serves me right for feeling so snooty, she told herself humbly. She had often noticed that it was just at those moments when she felt most pleased with herself that she stumbled, developed hiccups, or was told that her slip was showing.

"Shall I compare thee to a summer's day?
Thou art more lovely and more temperate. . . ."

There's another one, said Mona to herself. I don't care, I *do* think I'm pretty good. This time she was careful to look where she was going.

Rush's tree house was built in the branches of a strong oak on the hillside. Mona knew he was there because she could see one of his feet hanging over the side.

"Rush?"

"H-m-m?"

Mona climbed up the foot blocks to the tree house. Rush was lying flat on his back looking up at something.

"What are you doing?"

"Spotting," replied Rush without moving.

"*Spotting!* You couldn't even see a plane through all these leaves."

"Who said anything about spotting planes? I'm spotting woodpeckers."

"Oh. But what for?"

"I kind of like them. Especially the redheaded ones. They're so wise and sassy and make such a racket. They're always quarreling and forgetting about it, and when they lope up the sides of trees they look like spry old women with shawls on climbing up a ladder. And the noise they make when they drill! Regular tommy guns."

Mona looked up, too.

"I don't remember trees having quite so many leaves ever before."

"It always seems like that early in the summer," Rush said. "By the middle of July you get used to it."

"No, I think they change. Later they seem to shrink a little; they're not so fluffy. Oh, by the way, I came up to tell you those friends of yours, the Addisons, telephoned. They want to come over, so I said yes, and bring your bathing suits."

"Swell." Rush stood up, stretching. "It'll be good to get into the pool."

"It certainly will," agreed Mona with a sigh. "Gee, isn't it hot, though?"

The shade of William Shakespeare mocked her.

Randy, already in her bathing suit, was doing a dance on the lawn. She was circling one of the iron deer in a series of leaps and pirouettes; from time to time she knelt before it in an attitude of supplication.

"I'm Helen of Troy," she panted, as they went by. "And that's the Trojan horse."

"Helen of Troy!" exclaimed Rush. And Randy was rather hurt by the lengthy and violent manifestation of his mirth. After all, it wasn't so funny that he had to lie down on the grass and roll! But before there was time for reproaches the Addisons appeared. They had their bathing suits and towels tied into bundles on the ends of sticks.

"We're tramps!" shouted Daphne. "We're on our way to Alaska to pan gold!"

Then she saw Mona, and the shyness settled over her again. Over Dave, too.

"H'lo," he said, looking uncomfortable. "Gosh, hot, isn't it?"

"This is Mona, my other sister," Rush said, remembering his manners. "And I've got a brother somewhere, named Oliver, but I don't know where."

"Fishing, of course," Mona said. "That's all he ever does anymore."

Daphne was staring at Mona.

"We heard you on the radio in *The Penfold People*," she said at last. "My, were you ever good!"

"Sure were," Dave agreed.

Now it was Mona's turn to be shy. She was not quite used to being a radio star yet.

"Well, don't get her mixed up with Polly Penfold, though, just because she plays that role," cautioned Rush. "Polly's supposed to be kind of a misunderstood genius, or something. A grownup's idea of a smart kid that does dumb things. *You* know. But Mona's just ordinary. She isn't any genius or anything."

"No, she's just a nice, swell, everyday person," Randy agreed.

If Mona felt faintly nettled at having the glamour torn away from her so ruthlessly she didn't show it.

"I think I'll put on my bathing suit," she said. "Daphne,

you go with Randy, and Rush, you take Dave up to your room."

The swimming pool made friends of them. That pool was a blessing in every way. The Melendys were in and out of it all day long. It wasn't so very large. Even Oliver could swim the widest part in eleven strokes (or rather eleven dog paddles) and they were always having to pick caterpillars and dead hornets out of it, but at least it was water, and deep enough in one place to be above even Father's head.

Rush had built a springboard above this spot. He had worked with it until it snapped you into the air so briskly that your head almost flew from your shoulders. It was lovely.

Rush devoted hours of practice to his jackknife but had not yet succeeded in unfolding himself fast enough. Mona fancied herself doing a swan dive, and was pretty good at it, except that she almost always forgot to point her toes, which ruined the effect. Randy was just learning to dive, and spent hours determinedly hurting herself; but Oliver would have nothing to do with the springboard. He contented himself with belly-whoppers off the bank.

Dave Addison turned out to be a star swimmer. He could do a jackknife without forgetting to unfold in time, and a swan dive without forgetting to point his toes. He could do the crawl, the trudgeon, the butterfly breast stroke, and stay underwater longer than any of them. Mona and Rush were envious and admiring. They were fired with the zeal of competition. But Daphne was just about Randy's speed. They splashed together quietly, and talked as they swam.

Midges hung, gauzy flecks of gold, above the pool; the maple leaves were edged with light. Dragonflies hovered, sleeping on air, and were gone in a breath. The Melendys and their friends were water-sodden like old logs. All their skins were wrinkled, their nails were blue, their hair hung over their eyes in limp soaked strands, and they were perfectly happy.

"For heaven's sake, what's that?" Mona squinted, suddenly, through wet lashes at the driveway.

A boy was walking along it. Behind him trailed a small, dun-colored express wagon that had obviously had a long, eventful life: its wheels wobbled, and its sides were bent. In it were a tricycle, also aged with experience, a broken scythe, a lead fire engine, and an old-fashioned rattrap. The boy seemed to be a match for his possessions: barefooted, shirtless, he wore only a pair of faded overalls. His straw hat was frayed at the edges in a kind of brittle fringe. His arms were thin and long, and on each side of the crossed overall straps his shoulder blades stuck out in angles.

"It's Mark Herron!"

"He's brought the scrap!"

Randy and Rush were out of the pool, running to meet him, scattering water in the sunshine like sparrows leaving a puddle.

"Mark Herron!" exclaimed Daphne.

"Well, I'll be darned," said Dave. They both hung onto the bank and stared at the boy in the drive with their mouths open.

Mona frowned at them, mystified. "Mark Herron! Who's he?"

"He's a boy goes to our school," Daphne told her. "He hasn't any folks except a mean, terrible old cousin he has to live with."

"He's in my class," Dave said. "When he comes to school at all, he is."

"Why? Doesn't he like school?"

"Sure, but Oren, that's the cousin's name, he keeps him home to do the chores half the time. But he's smart! He doesn't have to study as hard as other people." Poor Dave looked rueful as he thought of his own defensive battles against arithmetic and spelling. "The teacher went down to see this cousin one day, over at his farm. Miss Schmidlapp, her name is, and she's real small. Well, she went driving down to Meeker's in her Ford coop, to talk about letting Mark come to school oftener. He chased her out of the house, Oren did. He chased her out yelling like a Comanche Indian, she told my mother, and he sicked the dogs on her, too. She got into her car fast as she could and slammed the door. And then she leaned out the window and told him what she thought of him, loud and quick. But there's still a dent in the back of her car where he threw a stove lid when she drove off."

"Yes, and so then they got the superintendent of schools after him. Mr. Ploutweaver." Daphne giggled. "He's an awful fat, big, serious man."

Dave giggled too, in spite of himself.

"*He* didn't even have time to get back in *his* car. He just ran, with the dogs on his heels, and it took him days to get his breath back. They had to send the constable down to drive the car out for him."

"Though it's awful to laugh, really." Daphne tried to look shocked at herself.

Meanwhile Randy and Rush were exclaiming enthusiastically over the scrap. You would have thought that Mark had brought a load of precious stones.

"Why, it's beautiful, just beautiful," gushed Randy, gazing fascinated at the rattrap.

"It was swell of you to lug it all that way," said Rush.

"Oh, that's nothing. Gee—" Mark said and waved his hat to finish the sentence. His glance stole briefly toward the swimming pool. Randy saw the dew of sweat on his upper lip, and the red damp pattern printed on his forehead by his hatband.

"Come and have a swim."

"Oh, I better be getting back home. Thanks just the same." Mark's bare feet shifted on the grass, and then paused as though they could not endure the thought of leaving.

"No, you stay; just for a dip. I'll lend you a suit," Rush insisted.

Mark hesitated, looked longingly at the pool, and turned to Rush with a smile.

"Well, okay. Just for a few minutes." This time his feet followed Rush's; quick, light, glad to go.

"So that's the Four-Story Mistake," he said, staring up at the house as they approached. "Sure looks nice."

"It's a good old dump." Rush sternly kept the pride out of his voice. "It's got it over the city like a tent."

"That little thing—that tower on top. I like that. All windows and a little roof. I bet it would be a wonderful place to sleep."

"Sometime maybe you can come and spend the night. You could sleep up there."

Mark's bright gaze wavered. "No, I guess I never could." Then he grinned again. "I'm sure glad to see it though. Say, why don't you and your sister come over on Wednesday? Would you? If it's not raining?" There was urgency in his voice.

"We'd like to," Rush said.

The Addisons were glad to see Mark, and he seemed glad that they were glad. He could swim all right, but had never tried to dive. Rush and Dave spent a happy, high-pitched hour instructing him in the rudiments of the art, while the girls dabbled and talked at the farther end of the pool. Daphne was telling them more about Mark in an undertone.

"His cousin treats him awful mean. Why, he hits him!" Daphne stared at them with appalled eyes. And they, treading water, stared back. "Once he came to school with a *black eye*! And he never has hardly anything to eat in his lunch pail. Dave used to try to give him some of his, but he's awful proud, Mark is. He almost always wouldn't take any. The kids all like Mark, they try to make friends with him, and he's real nice and everything, but after school he just kind of fades away. He won't ever go home with anybody or ask anybody to go home with him. We're all scared of his cousin and I guess he knows it.

"You know what he does, Oren? He locks Mark in his room at night when he's away. Mark told one of the boys and the boy told Dave and Dave told me. He locks him in but Mark knows a way to get out. He climbs out the window—"

Randy related all this to Rush a few minutes later when he swam up beside her. As she told him she kept staring at Mark with sorrowing eyes. There he was, a skinny boy in trunks, with his hair water-plastered to his head, holding his nose and running along the springboard. But she saw him as a martyr, a brave soul suffering in silence.

Rush splashed water at her. "Quit looking at him like that. I bet that's why he steered clear of the kids at school."

"Why? What are you talking about?"

"I bet he hates to be pitied. I bet if he thought we were going to get all mushy and pitying about him he'd steer clear of us, too."

"But, Rush, he has such a horrible time."

"Maybe he doesn't think of it like you do. People never feel pitiful to themselves. They feel sore, or mad, or blue or something; but they don't *ever* feel pitiful."

"How do you know?"

"I just know, that's all."

Randy accepted this as wisdom.

And afterward when they had come out of the pool and were playing on the lawn, and Mark was showing them how he could walk on his hands, the expression on her face was one of envious admiration. She could turn a perfect cartwheel herself, and Rush could stand on his head till he got purple in the face. But walking on the hands! That was something. Even Mona was impressed. Randy's heart swelled with respect as well as pity. Dave and Rush both tried to do it too, but though they got up all right they couldn't stay there. Randy and Daphne tried it. So did Mona. But none of them were any good. After a while they were so hot they had to go in the pool again.

"My lands!" shouted Cuffy from the house. "My lands! If you young ones don't come out soon you'll ooze water like sponges for the next three days. Come on out now, it's gettin' late, way past five."

"Past five!" Mark clambered onto the bank. "I'll have to hurry. I bet I've missed the milking. Oren will—"

But he didn't finish the sentence. He was running toward the house.

They all got out.

"We'll dress, too," Dave said. "Then we can walk up the road with Mark. Come on, Daff, make it snappy."

When they came down the children were so clean that they looked as if they'd been shellacked. There were wet drops on their collars from their soaked hair, and all their noses were red.

"So long, and thanks a lot," Mark said. And to Rush he added, "Remember Wednesday."

The Addisons became shy and formal again.

"Had a very nice time."

"Sure did."

They turned often and waved as they went up the drive.

"I like Mark," Mona said. "They're all nice, but Mark's the nicest."

Rush shook his head. "I hate to think of what he's going home to. A tanning, most likely, for missing the milking."

"Oh, Mona, if you could see where he lives!" said Randy. "A falling-to-pieces old house, and a falling-to-pieces old barn, with big, mean pigs all over the place, and big, mean dogs."

"And a big, mean cousin Oren," finished Rush.

"The whole thing sounds like Grimms' fairy tales," said Mona. "Almost too bad to be true."

"That's right," Rush agreed. "All the place needs is some bats, and cats, and buzzards; and a wicked step-mother cooking poison in a kettle."

"It couldn't be any worse even then," said Randy; and

Mona said, "We'll have to do something about him. We'll just have to think of *something*!"

They stood there on the lawn; each thinking about Mark.

"RUSH!" came an indignant voice from the front door. "You come right straight in and take your wet bathing trunks off your mantelpiece. Randy, go dry your hair! And, Mona, why aren't you setting the table?"

"Look out, Cuffy," warned Rush. "You sound as if you're studying to be a wicked stepmother. If you don't look out we'll give you to Oren Meeker."

"No, we will not!" Randy flew to the door where Cuffy was standing, and hugged her hard. "You're too good to us."

"Too good to you?" Cuffy was startled. She stroked Randy's head. "Gracious, child, your hair is sopping! Bring me your towel and I'll dry it myself."

Mona drifted languidly toward the house. *Her* head was effectively wound up in a turban of towel. As she walked she held her arm out in front of her and watched the sunlight glittering on the little hairs. Some words came into her mind.

> *"Three beauteous springs to yellow Autumn turn'd*
> *In process of the seasons have I seen,*
> *Three April perfumes in three hot Junes burn'd . . ."*

"Why, there's another one!" cried Mona triumphantly.

"There's another one, and I wasn't even looking for it."

Willy Sloper spoiled it though. At that moment he came around the corner of the house with a sack of laying mash over his shoulder.

"Hello there, Mona," said he. "Is it hot enough for you?"

CHAPTER IV

The Arrowhead

Wednesday was a beautiful day. The kind of day that is so clear that there is a blue edge to everything. The sun shining on the breakfast table turned the honey into such dazzling gold that one could hardly look at it. It even tasted golden. It tasted of summertime and sun and clover. It was a lovely thing to eat.

Mona kept yawning and staring out the window. She had a rose stuck in her hair, and it looked pretty.

"This is a special day," she said. "People ought to use it only for doing special things. I know what I'm going to do. I'm going up into the tree house and write a play; and after that I'm going to bake an angel cake without anyone helping me, and after *that*—well, I'll probably wash my hair."

"Building up to an anticlimax, all right," said Rush. "Randy and I really are going to do something special but it's a secret. What are you going to do, Oliver?"

"Fish," replied Oliver, scraping his egg.

"Need you ask?" Mona said. "He hasn't done anything else for the last ten days. But I suppose fishing is still the most important thing he knows about."

After breakfast Randy and Rush made a picnic lunch. Rush's sandwiches were massive untidy things, drippy with mayonnaise, and with pieces of lettuce hanging out like fringe, but Randy always preferred them to her own. They stuffed hard-boiled eggs, and took some milk in a thermos bottle. More than enough of everything for three people.

They rode recklessly down the road on their bicycles. The morning-lighted valley streamed past them, glittering, blazing with dew, alive with the sound of birds. Rush coasted down a hill with his arms folded and his feet on the handlebars; heaven knows why he didn't break his neck. Randy did nothing so dangerous; she had her mind on the picnic lunch in her basket. She was singing at the top of her lungs:

"Speed, bonny boat, like a bird on the wing
Over the sea to Skye!"

Oh, what a day! Randy had the feeling that if she just concentrated and pumped hard enough, her bicycle would take off, leave the earth entirely, and go soaring up into that dazzling sky. All too soon they came to Oren Meeker's crooked mailbox. It was in shadow; the trees hung still above the road, and suddenly they heard no birds.

Randy got off her bicycle. "It's kind of scary," she said, just as she had the first time they went up this road.

"Maybe it's because we know what kind of person lives here," Rush said.

They were quiet, wheeling their bikes up the hilly road. Wet timothy slapped against their overalled legs, and their sneakers were dark with dew, and sprinkled with grass pollen.

"I hope he's gone," Randy remarked nervously.

"Mental telepathy," said Rush. "I was just hoping the same thing."

"Maybe we ought to kind of hide in the bushes for a little while," suggested Randy, in a cowardly way. "One of us could go and reconnoiter." Rush gave her a cold, sideways look. "You mean *I* could go and reconnoiter. Thank you, no. Don't be a sissy, Miranda."

"Why, *I'm* not being a sissy," said Randy untruthfully. "I'm only being, you know, practical."

But it was all right, after all. They came up over the hill at last, and there lay Meeker's farm, desolate as ever, with no one in sight except Mark, who was cutting down yellow dock with a sickle.

As before, the great dogs sprang up from nowhere, and came flying toward them, all teeth and matted fur. Randy cowered behind Rush, who, if he did not cower, at least shielded himself behind his bike.

Mark shouted at the dogs, and they gave up the chase reluctantly; still sniffing at the Melendys and growling soft, crooning growls low down in their throats.

"Gee, I was afraid maybe you couldn't come," said Mark, flinging down the sickle and coming toward them smiling with delight.

"Has—uh—has Mr. Meeker gone?" Randy couldn't help asking.

"Oh, sure, 'bout an hour ago he went. Don't you worry; he won't be home till after dark."

"My sister is something of a sissy," Rush explained. "She's okay in other ways, though."

"What would you folks like to do first?" asked Mark, falling easily into the role of host.

"Arrowheads!" said Rush.

"Quarry!" said Randy.

"Why not both?" offered Mark. "You kids got your bathing suits?"

"Certainly," said Randy. "Right in my handlebar basket under the lunch. Lunch for all of us," she added hastily.

"You didn't need to bother about me." Mark looked proud. "Some days I don't even bother to eat dinner at all. I forget about it."

"Well, you shouldn't. Not while you're growing," said Randy severely.

"Listen to Grandma," jeered Rush. "The voice of experience!"

"She's probably right," said Mark peaceably. "Come on, let's get going."

They followed him past the decrepit barn with its odorous pigpen, up through a lean pasture with thistles sticking out of it, and then under a fence and into the woods on the hillside. As they climbed, the undergrowth became more and more matted and difficult. Blackberry canes and prickly ash were bound together with wild grapevines, clematis, and bittersweet. Fallen trees lay in ambush, their branches lifted like antlers. If the three children hadn't been wearing blue jeans their legs would have been scratched and torn to ribbons.

They did not talk much, the going was too difficult; they panted, and struggled, and ripped their way through the wilderness. Randy kept getting her hair caught on thorns, and Rush had a tear in his shirt.

Moths came fluttering up into the light, and so, unfortunately, did large, famished mosquitoes. But the children didn't mind any of it, there were so many interesting things to see: a wasp's nest like a big silver pear, a tree stump trimmed with fungus the color of tangerine peel. They saw a live walking stick, and some tiny orange lizards (efts, Mark said), and an owl sitting dazed on a branch. Between the damp, shaded roots of the trees there were mosses: cup moss and sealing wax; and on the boulders flat lichens were pressed in faded gray rosettes. They saw red toadstools, and yellow, and speckled, and flocks of little silver ones all crowded together. In the middle of a small clearing stood a solitary, exquisite white one, with a lining of palest pink.

"That's an amanita," Mark said almost in a whisper. "The destroying angel, they call it. One bite of that and you die in agony."

"Gee whiz," said Randy.

"You know a lot about things in the woods. Names and all," said Rush. "I wish you'd teach me some of them."

Mark was pleased. "I bet I don't pronounce 'em right, though. Sometimes when we go to Carthage I get a chance to go to the liberry; and Miss Schmidlapp, our teacher in school, told us about some of these things, and Oren's wife taught me a lot. But I still don't know more than a tiny little bit."

Finally they came out of the woods.

Just below the crest of the hill there was a barren stratum of sandstone, pitted with cliff swallows' caves, holes and pockmarks.

"Look out for snakes," Mark said. "There's rattlers around here." Seeing Randy's face, he added hastily, "But they're only puny ones, and awful shy besides."

Nevertheless Randy, and even Rush, stepped a little gingerly for the next five or ten minutes. After that they forgot about snakes.

The sandstone pockets were fascinating to explore. In some they found tiny paw prints, gnawed chokecherry pits, every evidence of small housekeeping but no sight of the housekeepers. In others, the highest ones, there were swallows' nests, many of them empty, since it was late in the season, but a few occupied by wide-mouthed fledglings or groups of eggs. Above, in the bright air, the parent swallows swooped in knife-sharp arcs and cried in fury and alarm.

"Let's leave the poor things alone," Mark said. "The arrowheads I found were mostly down below this cliff. Down among the loose rocks and sand that have chipped off during the years."

The spare grass was dry and scratchy there, and sandburs grew among the rubble. The mounting sun became stronger; it beat against the rocks. Drops of sweat rolled down Randy's forehead and dropped off, but she didn't mind. Poking with a stick among the pebbles and rocks she was as happy as an old gypsy on a trash heap.

And it was Randy who found the first arrowhead. The only one that day.

In a pleasant daze of heat and mild fatigue, she had been moving slowly along, not even poking, droning a tune without any words, and thinking about the sandwiches in the lunch basket. And suddenly there it was. Just lying there between the vervain flowers, sharp and definite as though printed on the rock. Randy had the feeling that she had been looking at it for several seconds without seeing it, and for a moment, now, she just stared at it without saying anything. Had she discovered a pigeonblood ruby, an amulet in the shape of Osiris, the diamond ring of an Infanta, she could not have been more stunned with joy.

When she spoke it was very quietly.

"I found one. I found an arrowhead. Gee whiz."

"Good for you!" said Mark.

"Swell!" said Rush.

They hurried over to see. There it lay in the palm of her hand, clear-cut and shining. It felt cool against her skin, and in the sunlight it glittered like sugar.

"White flint, and a beauty," Mark said. "A good-sized one, too."

"Golly, that's neat, Ran." Rush was nearly as pleased as she. "Come on, kids, let's see if we can't find some more."

He and Mark returned to their poking and prodding, but not Randy. She did not wish to cloud the moment by further searching. Two arrowheads would have been less perfect than one. She sat on a patch of ground that was free from sandburs and looked at her treasure. She gazed at it glittering on the palm of her hand. She tried it against the blue denim of her overalled leg; it looked fine there, too. Then she placed it on the ground, glanced away, turned back again casually, pretending to see it for the first time. The shock of delight was nearly as good as the first.

She tried to imagine the Indian who had carved this pointed stone to tip his arrow. She pictured him first as an old chief, with a face like a dried apricot, a full war bonnet, a feather cloak, and a name like Great Laughing Paw. She could see him, too, as a redskin boy of about Rush's age, with dark, long hair and white teeth. A future chief. The Hiawatha type. But the picture she preferred was that of a maiden, a beautiful creature of about twelve, dressed entirely in white doeskin, with a single white feather in her hair. Little Birch Bark, or Lone Swan, something like that: an adventurous spirit who refused to sit at home weaving and cooking with the other squaws; who wandered, instead, white as a wraith by the edge of the lake at night, carrying her bow and arrow and singing a strange, haunting melody— At this point Randy sighed. It would be a poor huntress, for heaven's sake, who stalked her prey singing at the top of her lungs; besides, there wasn't any lake for miles around. Randy was shamefacedly aware that Little Birch Bark's place was on the cover of sheet music, or on a drugstore calendar, and not in the history of this valley.

"What kind of Indians lived around here, Mark?" she called.

"The tough ones. The Iroquois. They're s'posed to have had a battle here in this valley a long time ago. That's how come all the arrowheads."

Great Laughing Paw, Hiawatha, and Little Birch Bark all melted away forever. Instead, a newcomer emerged in

Randy's mind: a stranger with a savage, hawk-nosed face and paint-striped cheeks. Someone who wore only a loincloth and moccasins, and whose hair stood up in a narrow crescent over his cropped skull. She could imagine him moving through the woods, all in one piece like an animal, noiseless, intent, never aimless. She could not imagine him smiling. Randy looked at the arrowhead with new respect. She was glad that this was all she need ever know of its creator.

"I'm hot," said Rush, hurling himself down on the ground, and at once hurling himself upright again with a bellow that would have done credit to the bloodiest Iroquois. "Jeepers! Sandburs!" He came limping over to Randy and stood pathetically while she picked them out of his trouser legs and sneakers.

"Burs I could do without," said he. "Also gravel roads when I'm barefoot. Also thistles (except that they look okay); also stinging jellyfish, beetles, splinters, and all hot-tasting things like horseradish. Quick, Ran, you name some things you could do without. No deep thoughts, you know, just troublesome everyday things you don't like."

"Arithmetic," said Randy, like a shot. "And cucumbers, and taking ticks off dogs, and washing dishes, and having snarls combed out of my hair, and being sick at my stomach, and starch in the collars of my dresses, and—shall I go on?"

"No, it's Mark's turn. Quick, Mark, don't think first, just say 'em."

"Well—uh. Weeds like quack grass and pussley. Spreading manure. Getting up before it's light on winter mornings. Hens. Mosquitoes. Oren."

There was a little silence. Mark looked embarrassed. "Well, I just did like you said: said 'em without thinking."

"Is he so awful to you?" asked Randy at last.

"Meaner'n a rattlesnake," said Mark, and then laughed. He didn't want to talk about it anymore. "What do you say we go to the quarry now? A swim might be nice."

"Yes, and then lunch," Randy said, rejoicing that they had brought such a big one.

They plowed along the ridge another mile and then down the other side through a shoulder-high jungle of hazel bushes; up another hillside and there they were.

The quarry had steep walls of rough marble, and held within them was a pool, a little pond, deep, brimming with pure spring water. It was dark and smooth and clear, like a shield made of obsidian, and it held upon its surface a distinct picture of all that surrounded and framed it: sky with a cloud in it, the black juniper clusters, arched spears of birch, three children looking down.

"Deep," Rush said.

"You bet. Thirty feet, they say. Cold, too."

"Boy, I can hardly wait to get in it!"

The boys disappeared behind a rock, and Randy found

some juniper bushes for a dressing room: very scratchy.

"It seems a shame to mess it up," Randy remarked, looking at the motionless pool, when they had emerged in their bathing suits.

Rush took the first dive. For a split second he could see himself, reflected in the flawless surface, arched in space; blue sky behind him. Not a bad dive, Rush complimented himself before he struck. In that instant all thought was gone. Nothing remained but the breathless upward struggle through liquid ice. He came out like the cork of a champagne bottle and clawed himself onto the bank.

"Ho-ly cat!"

"Cold?" inquired Randy.

"Cold! Holy cat!" was all Rush could say.

"Spring water, that's why," Mark explained. "When you go in the second time it won't feel so bad, and the third time is always swell."

Randy belonged to the toe-dipping, squealing school. She went through this performance for quite a long time, and only the disgusted comments of her brother Rush forced her to go in at all.

"You're acting like one of those old-time bathing beauties," he said. "You ought to be wearing stockings and carrying a parasol."

"Rush, you're a beast. I'm not like that at all!" With this Randy plunged inelegantly; holding onto her nose and stepping out into space as desperately as a man walking the plank.

The third time, as Mark had prophesied, was the best. They no longer felt paralyzed. They felt warm, exhilarated, endowed with superhuman strength. They yelped, splashed, tumbled, and ducked.

Randy had never been so far beyond her depth before. She swam straight across the pool full of power and daring. As she swam she encountered an occasional floating leaf; an occasional struggling fly or beetle. Each fly or beetle she rescued and set upon a leaf boat to dry his soaked wings and legs. It gave her a feeling of virtue to do this. She could imagine all heaven looking down upon her and approving. Notice Miranda Melendy; she is a kind, generous girl. The smallest insect is not too unimportant to receive her charitable attention. She ought to be rewarded. Randy thought of the arrowhead complacently, probably that in itself was a reward. She swam back again with a smile of sweet unselfishness; a misty radiance about her bathing-capped head.

"Why do you swim with your head way out like that?" inquired Rush, who was sitting on a ledge. "You're even *swimming* like an old-time bathing beauty. And why are you grinning that goonish way?"

Randy grabbed her brother's ankle and yanked him in again. Naturally Rush ducked her. Naturally she ducked Rush. Naturally Rush—and so on and so on. Heaven ceased to contemplate Miranda Melendy and went about its business, and Randy's halo fell off and was lost in thirty feet of water.

They sat side by side on a ledge with only their feet in the water and watched their goose flesh subside.

"I feel as if there's ginger ale instead of blood in my veins," said Rush. "And, oh, brother, am I hungry."

Mark looked away absentmindedly as if he felt it would be wrong to admit that he was hungry when he had nothing to contribute. Nevertheless, they had little difficulty in coaxing him to eat three of Rush's noble sandwiches, two stuffed eggs, an orange, and numberless cookies.

Afterward they just sat and scorched in the sun for a while. Then they swam again. It was even colder now, for the pool's surface was in shadow. Without the sunlight it looked deeper, more somber, more dangerous.

Mark took them home by a different route. It was just as tangled as the last, and just as interesting. He introduced them to the taste of sassafras and black birch twigs; and to the various fragrances of pennyroyal, and bee balm, and prickly ash.

"My nose feels very well exercised," Randy said. "It's learned a lot in the last half hour."

They came to a clearing.

"Here," said Mark, "this is what I wanted to show you."

Square blocks of stone lay cluttered on the ground, half buried in weeds, and from their midst rose a stout brick chimney with a fireplace in it, and close by, leaning toward the chimney, grew a lilac bush, almost a tree, tall, unkempt, with dead branches showing among its heart-shaped leaves.

"A house," said Randy wonderingly. "Here in this wild place, a house, or the shell of one."

"Whose was it?" Rush wanted to know.

"Who can tell? It fell to pieces, or burned up, years and years ago. Maybe fifty, maybe a hundred."

Maybe fifty, maybe a hundred.

There were flowers in the tangle of undergrowth and scattered stones: small patches of white and faded pink.

"Look," cried Randy. "Phlox! All gone small and puny because of weeds, but still growing!"

"Yes, and the lilac bush comes out in spring," Mark told her. "You can smell it way down at the foot of the hill; and the lilies of the valley have spread all back through the woods. You can see their leaves. . . . And look, those are apple trees, see? Mostly dead wood, and the apples are kind of small, but they sure taste good."

He showed them a mourning dove's nest in the lilac bush, and swifts' nests, made of mud, inside the chimney. He showed them the two deep doorways, one for entrance, one for escape, belonging to the woodchuck who was the present tenant of the house. He showed them the well, and they leaned over the stone rim and looked down into it and saw the still water far below, like black ink in a bottle, and the dark reflection of their three heads, and the thick fur of green moss clinging to the stones. Rush dropped a pebble in, and they waited, without breathing, for the splash, the little, hollow, echoing, empty plop.

"It has a special sound," Randy said. "As if it was saying that this is the first pebble anyone has dropped into it in a hundred years!"

Mark did not tell her that he himself had dropped dozens of pebbles into that well and that they always made the same sound.

"I love this place," said Randy. "Let's all come up here for a picnic sometime. Maybe when the apples are ripe."

After that they went home. Mark had to hurry because it was almost milking time, and he had other neglected chores to take care of before Oren came home.

"It's been a perfect day," Randy said, pressing her hand against the arrowhead in her pocket. "Can we come again next Wednesday?"

"You bet your life," said Mark wholeheartedly, and looking very happy.

As they coasted down the road to home Rush said, "I think he's a swell guy, don't you?"

And Randy replied, "Next to you and Oliver he's the nicest boy I ever saw. And he's the *only* one I ever saw that could walk on his hands and knew the names of toadstools."

It was good to be home again; they felt as if they had been gone for days. Mona looked beautiful, and knew it. Her freshly washed hair lay in a cloud about her shoulders, and in honor of this she had put on her only long dress; the one she had worn to her first dance in the spring, and in her hair, of all things, she had fastened a whole strawberry plant, leaves, fruit, blossoms.

"Why not the roots, too?" Oliver wanted to know, when they all sat down to supper. And Rush said, "This year the Sub Deb or Junior Miss will wear fruit in her hair. Next year she will wear vegetables: kohlrabi, a wreath of Brussels sprouts, or a single full-blown parsnip. The year after that—"

But Mona wouldn't rise to the bait. She just laughed. She knew exactly how becoming the strawberries were, and shook her head a little to make them dangle against her cheek.

Randy just stared at her, forgetting to wipe the milk from her upper lip, and earnestly hoping with all her heart that someday when she was old like Mona she would be half as pretty. That would be a nice wish to have granted, thought Randy, remembering heaven. But after supper, playing Any Over with Rush and Oliver and Willy, she decided that she would rather be granted the ability to throw a ball like a boy.

When she went to her room that night the first thing she saw was the arrowhead shining under the lamp on her bedside table. She took it up in her hand and thought of the day, the wonderful day with Mark and Rush: the woods, the lost house, the marble quarry pool, the cliff swallows. She knew that she would always remember it.

She got into bed feeling a little uncomfortable about the way she'd been instructing heaven how to reward her. Why, it had been giving her the best it had to give the whole day long.

And an arrowhead thrown in.

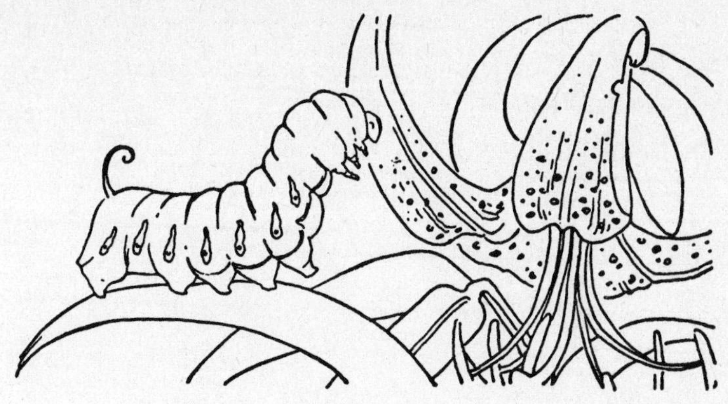

CHAPTER V

Oliver's Other World

"Fish and caterpillars. Caterpillars and fish. They're the things that Oliver lives for," said Rush wearily, one Saturday at lunch. "This is the third time we've eaten chub this week, and all because Oliver's learned how to fish."

"Free and unrationed," said Cuffy severely. "*And* nourishing."

"Be glad it's the fish we have to eat and not the caterpillars," suggested Mona.

Oliver looked up dreamily. "You *can* eat caterpillars,

you know. African savages do; I read about it in a book. Big white grubs they eat. I wonder if—"

"Well, you can just stop wondering, my friend," Father interrupted. "We're not savages, at least not authorized ones; we're the softened products of civilization, thank heaven, and our diet doesn't include the larvae of Lepidopterae. At least not yet. Probably the day will come when they'll be found a most valuable source of vitamin Q, and we'll eat them every day as a matter of course along with our green, leafy vegetables."

"Ugh," said Mona, shuddering fastidiously but going right on eating.

"Chub!" said Rush, taking a bone out of his mouth. He made the word sound like a swear. "Chub, chub, chub, chub, chub! All summer long nothing but chub. Baked, grilled, fried in meal. Oliver, couldn't you please, just once, catch a trout, or even an eel?"

But Oliver wasn't listening. He was thinking about something else. There was mashed potato on his chin, and a dash of jelly on his cheek, but his eyes looked into a distance of their own and saw something which made them shine with a grave contentment.

It was true that during the past month he had been making an exhaustive study of the two subjects, caterpillars and fish. They were the twin enthusiasms of his scientific nature. Just now the insects were a little in the lead.

Oliver wondered how he had lived so long without pay-ing any real attention to caterpillars. It seemed a terrible oversight. Perhaps it was because he had never before lived in a place where caterpillars were so abundant. Here, in the gardens and woods, they were everywhere. Small and green, they swung themselves down from the trees on threads, and got caught in your hair, or were discovered hours later inching themselves along your collar. "Measuring you for a new suit of clothes," Willy said. And then, of course, there were the tent caterpillars in their ugly pavilions of soiled gossamer; and the furry kind, red or black, such as there are everywhere, always ruffling busily along the roads, or up and down stalks. Oliver, like any other child, had patted the furry ones, stepped on the tent ones, and felt a cold flicker of repulsion when he picked one of the thread-swingers off his collar. Otherwise they had never occupied his thoughts.

All this was changed, however, one morning in mid-July. One day, impersonating a Sherman tank, he was bellowing and threshing his way among some of the shrubs near the summer house, when he came face to face with an extraordinary thing. It was something which looked like a tiny, elaborate trolley car. It was perched on a leaf, standing firmly on ten blunt little round feet that could have been wheels; and, exactly like the connecting rod on a surface car, a sort of horn or antenna stuck up at one end of it (Oliver decided the hind end, the thing was probably a tail). The other end was raised defiantly, and Oliver thought he discerned a sort of face there. The whole creature was a rich cinnamon brown color, and along each of its velvety sides was arranged an ornamental row of creamy scrolls.

"Gee," breathed Oliver, and stuck his finger out in front of the fantastic thing. "I never saw one as big as this, or as fancy! Come here and let me look at you."

At that the caterpillar rippled forward, exactly as if it had understood each word, raised itself up again and placed its two front—what would you call them—paws? Feet? Hands?—right on Oliver's grass-stained finger. Oliver held his breath. He had never been so flattered in his life.

That was the beginning of his new passion. After that came a long period of collecting. Caterpillars of every type were brought home by Oliver to be housed in Mason jars, jelly jars, milk bottles, and any other transparent receptacle that could be appropriated without too much hue and cry. (Cuffy had thought of several things to say when she discovered the cabbage caterpillars in her best glass baking dish). There was a different specimen in every jar, along with a generous supply of whatever they had been eating when Oliver had found them.

Cuffy and Mona protested strenuously, but Rush and Randy were eager collaborators, and even Father said, "It's a good interest for a boy. He can learn a lot about human progress by watching caterpillars."

Unwillingly resigned, Cuffy cut out rounds of mosquito

netting to put over the jars, and Mona tied them on with different colored bits of worsted.

"There," she said to each one, as she pulled the fastening tight. "Stay in there, now, till you turn into something less revolting: a butterfly or moth."

Nevertheless, somehow or other, in their sly, insinuating way, the creatures often managed to escape, and from time to time there were shrieks from some member of the family.

"Cuffy! There's a caterpillar in my hat!" Or, "Oliver! One of your rotten old worms is building a cocoon in my hairbrush. Come and take him aw-a-a-y!"

At times like these Oliver preferred to leave the house quietly and rapidly till the storm had blown over. After a while the rest of the family learned to bear their cross with patience and finally even with a sort of enthusiasm. It happened occasionally that Oliver forgot to feed his pets. It was hard to keep up with them. Heavens, how they ate! Leaves, stems, everything they could get their industrious jaws on. It was as if a growing boy in one day ate nine Thanksgiving dinners. Oliver had to fill the jars first thing in the morning and last thing at night, and the night feeding was the one he liked to forget. This meant that often his pets would be found striding ravenously about in their glass prisons, or trying to push off the mosquito netting in order to widen their frantic search for food.

"Oh, for Pete's sake!" Rush would groan. "The parsley caterpillar's finished the parsley again. He's gobbled up a bale already. I suppose I'll have to get it some more."

Or Mona would push open the kitchen door. "Cuffy, have you got a cabbage leaf? The disgusting cabbage caterpillars are all out of their disgusting cabbage."

Even Father, upon occasion, was to be seen flickering gloomily about the garden with a flashlight to get "more lilac leaves for the confounded cecropia larva." After all, he had encouraged this hobby.

When the caterpillars had eaten several hundred times their own weight in greenstuff they began making cocoons. In each glass jar Oliver had put some earth or a strong twig, depending on whether the creature in question was a burrower or a weaver. Even Cuffy and Mona found themselves interested in the progress of the cocoons: they were so ingenious, beautifully knitted, and in some cases lovely to look at. The monarch caterpillar, for instance, contrived a waxy chrysalis of pale green, flecked with tiny arabesques of gilt. It hung from the twig on a little black silk thread, like the jade earring of a Manchu princess.

"How lovely!" cried Mona. "Oh, if there were only some way of preserving them. I'd like to have a pale-green dress all buttoned down the front with those."

Oliver was outraged, and Rush said, "There's a woman for you. Always thinking of the beauties of nature in terms of wearing apparel. Can't see a shiny spider web without wanting to make a snood out of it. Can't see the Grand Canyon without wanting to dye something to match it. Can't—"

"Oh, Rush, if you could hear how stuffy you sound!" cried Mona. "Pompous and stuffy and about fifty years old. I suppose you'd rather have me quote a poem!"

"Well, you never lost an opportunity yet," Rush observed. "What's the matter, didn't Shakespeare ever write any poetry about cocoons?"

The nice thing about the monarch chrysalis was that the creature which emerged at the end of two weeks was as beautiful as his case. Orange-red and cream and black, like the petals of a tiger lily, he clung to the twig till his wings dried and widened, and then Oliver took him to the open window and deposited him gently on a leaf. Watching the butterfly fluttering away in the sunshine Oliver could not help feeling a little like God releasing a new soul into the world.

Cocoons kept turning up in the queerest places. A few caterpillars had inevitably escaped and Cuffy was loud in her protests at finding two little silk hammocks clinging to the living-room baseboard, another stuck to Father's typewriter, and another jade earring dangling from the dining-room ceiling.

"Gives you the creeps," she grumbled, "to imagine them things prowling around the house like they owned it, and building their nests any old place."

"Cocoons or chrysalises, *not* nests," said Oliver firmly,

and was grateful that though she grumbled Cuffy did not destroy the cocoons.

Oliver was having a wonderful summer. He loved it all. Fish, insects, swimming pool, woods, his own bicycle. What more could a boy ask?

Yet Oliver did have something more. He had a secret world that he entered when he went to bed. A world of which his family had no idea, Cuffy least of all. And it was by no means the world of dreams.

On the nights when he was not immediately claimed by sleep, and when he was reasonably sure of not being discovered, Oliver would sit up in his bed, turn on his flashlight and point it at the window. The effect was instantaneous and rewarding.

Out of the thick, night woods in the valley the moths came, flying in hundreds, fascinated by the shining eye of Oliver's window. As if attached to threads they were drawn by the light; clouds of them, swarms of them, fluttering out of the dark. And with them came all kinds of beetles; as well as the midges and mosquitoes which were small enough to crawl through the screen's meshes. Oliver didn't care, though. He slapped and scratched absently, and stared at the moths. He never tired of watching them, they were so beautifully made, with their patterned wings, tiny fur jackets, and dark, blank eyes. Up and down, up and down the screen they walked on tiny legs, their wings trembling. Others thumped and knocked against the broad overhanging eaves, and still others kept emerging from the shadows, soaring and drifting, like lazy confetti or blown petals in the dark. And now in Oliver's room a sound could be heard: a whispering, a rustling, of hundreds of small, soft wings.

Oliver sat transfixed and spoke quietly from time to time, telling himself the names of the ones he knew. "There's a Virgin Tiger moth," he'd say confidingly. "There's a nice Sphynx, very nice," or "Oh, boy, what a swell Leopard." When an interesting one came along that he didn't know, it was necessary for him to get out of bed, find the moth book and look it up. Really, with all this nocturnal scientific research, Oliver got very little sleep.

Sometimes a big hawk moth would appear, clinging to the screen. His eyes were little, fierce flecks of fire, and his fringed antennae were like tiny ferns or feathers. His wings vibrated so rapidly that they became a humming mist. There he would cling, in love with the light, staring at it, longing to reach it. Why? Oliver wondered. What did the light mean to them all?

Sometimes a big beetle would come, blasting and intoning, repeatedly hurling himself so hard against the screen that often he fell over on his back on the windowsill, and lay there for twenty minutes at a time, grappling the air with frantic, spurred legs. He never learned.

"Nitwit," Oliver would say to him contemptuously. "Thundering around that way isn't going to get you anyplace."

Danger also lurked beyond the window. Suddenly, darting up from nowhere, savage and swift, would come a bat. For a split second Oliver could see its tiny snout and mouse's ears, as it pursued the larger moths. His heart never failed to give a little skip when he saw it, for now, to him, the scene framed by his window had enlarged, become enormous. The moths had changed from moths into animals, or people, or fantastic beings from another world; and the bat was no longer a bat, it was instead the devil himself, or an ogre among gauzy innocents, or a black panther in a jungle. Oliver, watching, had become moth-sized, too, and felt a thrill of absolute terror when the bat appeared. It was exciting, and he shivered as he looked. The flashlight dramatically illuminated all these activities beyond the window.

One night after he had turned off the flashlight and lain down to sleep, and had just begun working on a dream, he was aware of a sound. At first he heard it reluctantly; far away, a gentle interruption which persisted. At last he opened his eyes and concentrated on listening. It was a velvety sound, very soft, like the pat, pat, pat, of a little felt slipper on the eaves. "A moth and a pretty good-sized one, too," said Oliver, sitting up fast, interested as any hunter stalking his prey. He pointed the flashlight at the window and turned it on. Instantly the small insects which had been asleep on the screen woke up and began their tireless promenading up and down, always up and down, in their ceaseless search for an entrance. Pat, pat, pat, just out of sight the mysterious one bumped gently against the eaves. Oliver held the light temptingly close to the screen, willing the stranger to appear. And presently he was rewarded.

Floating out of the dark, knocking against the overhang, came something so beautiful, so fairylike that Oliver hardly dared to breathe. The thing was a moth, but like no other moth that he had seen. Its wings were as wide as his two hands opened out, as frail as a pair of petals, and colored a pale, pale green: a moonlit silvery green.

"Gee," whispered Oliver. He sat there staring. "A luna! I never thought I'd see a real luna!"

It came close, hovered against the screen, and paused there. He could see the long curved tails on its wings, the delicate white fur on its body and legs. Oliver thought he had never seen anything so perfect. He and the moth watched each other for a long moment; neither moved.

Then suddenly, sharp, quick, dark against darkness, up came the bat. Oliver jumped to his feet, clapping his hands, and shouting.

"Get out of here, bat! You get away, you get away!"

With a sound like the flutter of a candle flame the bat departed. But Oliver knew it would be back again. With his finger he tapped gently against the screen where the moth was clinging.

"Go away now, luna," he said to it. "Go away fast, go home to the jungle where the panther won't get you."

The moth fluttered away from the screen, reluctant and

bewildered. Oliver put out the light so that it would go back where it belonged: back to the mysterious, leafy place from which it had come.

Pat, pat, pat went the little felt slipper under the eaves. Pat, pat, pat, and then silence. Oliver looked out. He could just see the great, pale creature floating toward the woods, drifting away on the tides of darkness like a flower on a pool.

There was a sudden sound. Light came into the room; Oliver turned guiltily.

"Oliver Melendy!" Cuffy's voice sounded queer without her teeth. "What *are* you doing? Was that you a minute ago, clappin' and hollerin'?"

"It was me," admitted Oliver, climbing back into bed and pulling the sheet up over himself and the hundred-odd little midges that had crept in through the meshes of the screen. "I was just scaring away a black panther."

"Black panther!" scoffed Cuffy. "It's all them doughnuts you ate. Milk of mag for you tomorrow, young man."

Even the thought of Milk of Magnesia failed to diminish the triumphant joy of the last few minutes. Instead of the usual groans of protest which met such an announcement, Oliver turned upon Cuffy a smile of radiant good will. "Okay, thanks. Good night," said he, and Cuffy left the room with a puzzled look.

For a long time after that whenever he thought about the luna moth he felt happy. He was careful not to think of it too often. Just once in a while he would look into his own mind and let himself see it again: his discovery, his beautiful guest, his secret. Seeming more than a moth, it paused there at his window: rarest green, fragile, perfect, living. The thought of it made Oliver happy all over again.

This is what he was remembering that day at lunch, with the mashed potato on his chin, the dash of jelly on his cheek, and the wondering contentment in his eyes.

CHAPTER VI

The Citronella Peril

One day Rush went to see Mark by himself. Randy couldn't come; she had to go to the dentist in Braxton, and had departed glowering with rage, disappointment, and apprehension. Also she clung to the unreasonable conviction that Rush shouldn't have gone to see Mark without her. He should have stayed home.

But Rush couldn't see it that way. He'd only have half a day with Mark anyhow, as the morning had all been squandered mowing the lawn.

Isaac wanted to go too, but Rush wouldn't let him. "Meeker's dogs would make hamburger out of you. You stay home. Good boy, Isaac, good old lop-eared boy." But Isaac refused to be mollified. He tucked the side of his lip between his teeth, which was his way of sulking, and glared at Rush with eyes like hot molasses. And he decided to go away by himself. He'd show them. John Doe (who was more Willy's dog than anyone's) tried to dissuade him, but got nowhere. Isaac went trotting off toward the woods by himself, looking for trouble.

Rush whistled as he rode. This time he carried a bucket, as well as the picnic basket, on his handlebars.

"I know where there are blackberries as big as *that*," Mark had said. "Only wear long pants, because, boy, are they thorny."

Rush wore blue jeans and heavy shoes. So did Mark. But the day was so hot that they took off their shirts and left them under the chokecherry tree above the farm with the picnic basket.

"Look," said Rush, with pride, "I brought some citronella."

"What's that?"

"Stuff to keep the mosquitoes off. Here, smell."

"Pew! I'd rather be bit."

"Oh, no, you wouldn't. You get used to it by and by, and it really works."

Both boys slathered themselves liberally.

The afternoon progressed satisfactorily. Mark took Rush to new woods; he seemed to know them all like the palm of his hand. The blackberries were almost as large as he had said. For a long time the boys wandered among the brambles, pulling the juicy berries from their clusters, and eating as many as they dropped in their buckets. The branches above dipped in the summer wind; the woods were full of drifting light and shade. There were emerald-green cushions of moss between the oak roots; Mark found a tree toad clinging to the bark of a birch, and Rush found a puffball as big as his head. Woodpeckers drummed on dead wood, and somewhere not far away there were crows calling, "kr-a-a-a, kr-a-a-a, kr-a-a-a." They sounded ancient and contentious, like money-changers in the Bible. Rush felt as if he were a thousand miles away from civilization, and he enjoyed the feeling.

"Pretend this is Guadalcanal," he said. "Those crows are Japs. Their camp is over there somewhere. We're Marines, of course. We have no communications, we're absolutely on our own. A volunteer job at great risk. We have to find this encampment and spy on it. You understand Japanese, see, and you tell me everything they're saying, and I take it down in shorthand."

Mark caught on at once. "Can't be too careful," he murmured earnestly. "They may have sentries posted anywhere—"

"Yes, and booby traps, maybe. They're clever, you know. Mustn't underestimate 'em."

"We're without food and water, too. We have to eat these berries. They're not blackberries. They're—they're—"

"The fruit of the Weehawken tree. An Oriental tree. We're lucky to have found them."

The berries had an extraordinary savor after that. They simply stuffed them; there was purple all around their mouths.

"You be Jefferson and I'll be McBride," said Rush. "Quiet now, Jefferson, we're getting closer."

"Lie down, McBride! A Zero overhead!"

They flung themselves down so hard that Jefferson said, "Ow," in a loud, normal voice.

"Sh-h-h," hissed McBride, "see, there he goes!" A hawk floated lazily against the sky.

"A near thing, Jefferson, a near thing. Better take it easy from here on."

As they crept, bent forward, the sounds of the enemy came clearer. The boys were so intent on the game, and so quiet in its performance, that they leapt with dismay when a startled partridge beat its way out of their path.

They came to a clearing, crawled under some hazel bushes, and found themselves looking down at a farm in a valley. It stood among cornfields like an island at sea, and above these fields the enemy was hovering.

"All right, Jefferson, let's have it."

And for the next fifteen minutes Jefferson, in a low, tense whisper, interpreted the crows to McBride, who gravely wrote the message upon the palm of his hand with a hazel twig.

At the end McBride arose with a strange, quiet smile.

"Here you are, Jefferson, take the message back to the commanding officer. I rather think that news about the reinforcements may be useful to him. So long, old man."

"Why? What the heck, aren't you coming too?"

McBride shook his head and winced a little. "They got me, pal," he said, and died; very cleverly, with a spiral twist like in the movies.

Mark was admiring. "Gee, I never would have thought of that. You did it good, too."

Rush waved aside the compliment. "I'm hungry, aren't you? And the basket's way back near the farm."

"I have to milk first. Come on; you help me get in the cows and I'll give you a lesson."

Rush had a new respect for Mark after the milking lesson.

"Why, I thought it would be just like turning on a faucet," he said in amazement. "Nothing to it, that's what I thought. Just a simple twist of the wrist."

"That's what everybody thinks until they try."

Mark gave the lean black cow a loving swat on its hindquarters and picked up the bucket.

Next they fed the pigs, collected hens' eggs, finished up the dozen-odd chores that Mark left till the last minute on his precious Wednesdays. By the time they climbed the hill to the chokecherry tree the sun was already setting, and they were famished. They did not speak while they were eating, they were too hungry. They simply sat there, chewing, and watched the sun go down. It left its light behind it long after it had gone; the western sky was a flood of gold. The swallows came up into the air, their wings as sharp as scissors; and before the swallows had left the bats too had begun to fly. At first it was difficult to tell which was which, they both swooped and fluttered, and zigzagged and curved with the same reckless style.

"Aerobatics," said Rush. "Unless I'm mistaken that bat just did a perfect Immelmann."

"What the heck is that?"

"A kind of loop the loop, I believe," replied Rush, who really was not sure, but who liked the sound of the word "Immelmann."

The two boys lay on their backs on the hillside, full of food and peace. Below in the hollow, the dreary farm was drowned by the dusk. Now and then one of the Meeker dogs barked: they had deep, hollow voices, that always sounded as if they were barking in a cellar. Overhead, the sky was gradually filled with stars.

"Watch," said Mark mysteriously. "I predict that within five minutes you will see a shooting star. Before half an hour's up you will have seen at least twenty or twenty-five."

Rush laughed. "I hope you sent your order in early."

"Don't worry," said Mark, still mysterious. "I fixed it up for you. Just keep watching, and you'll see."

Rush lay idly staring up at the sky and all its thousand points of light. Suddenly one of them sped across the dark, bright as a firefly, but sure of its goal as a bird.

Rush sat up abruptly. "Say!"

Mark smiled. "Lie down; keep watching."

Almost at once there was a second star-flight, and a third. A prickle of superstition crept over Rush's scalp.

"Come across, now; what's the secret?"

"When you've counted twenty-five I'll tell you."

"There's something very fishy about this," growled Rush. Long before the half hour was up he had counted twenty-five.

"Okay, come clean."

"Well, I kind of hate to. For a minute I almost thought I was running the show. But it's only because it's the eleventh of August."

Rush was still mystified.

"I don't get it."

"Didn't you ever hear about the Perseids?"

"No. What are they?"

"They're the shooting stars you've been looking at. Every August they come, the sky is full of them. Specially around the tenth. I've counted more'n a hundred some nights."

"I never knew that. Look, there goes another!"

"Lots of shooting stars come again around the middle of November, the Leonids, but somehow I always forget to look for them then."

"Gee, I learn more from you than I learn in a whole year at school," said Rush admiringly, and Mark was more than happy to hear these words of praise.

"I learn a lot from you, too," he said. He wanted to say: I've learned what it's like to have a friend, but of course he didn't because he was afraid of sounding sappy.

Mark knew the constellations too. He showed Rush (who didn't know anything except the Big Dipper) the patterns of Cassiopeia's Chair, and Scorpio. For a long time they wandered together in the glittering meadows overhead.

Rush came back to earth first.

"I'd better go—"

"What's the matter, why?"

"Well, I wouldn't like you to get in trouble. Oren wouldn't like to find me here," Rush said, and added candidly, "and I wouldn't want him to."

"He doesn't come home till late Wednesday nights. Honest." Mark sat up suddenly. "Would you like to know why? I could show you. Come on, Rush. Only you must promise never to tell."

"I promise," said Rush, curiosity winning, as usual. "Tell me what it is."

"No, I'll show you. Come on."

"But where?"

"Up the hill a ways. In the woods."

"Well, okay, but let's put some more citronella on. The mosquitoes have found out about us."

They crawled under the fence again and crossed the pasture. There was a smell of pennyroyal. The woods were very dark ahead.

"What can Oren be doing in the middle of the pitch-black woods at night?" Rush wondered aloud. "He could be hunting possums, except they don't have 'em around here. He could be collecting moths, but it's not very likely. He could be operating a counterfeiting machine (much more likely), or hiding stolen money, or lying in wait for an enemy (he probably has quite a number), or—"

"Tisn't any of those," Mark said. "Though it's against the law, all right."

They were in the woods now, and creeping through the undergrowth. Rush, at Mark's heels, wondered how he could find his way so easily. The dense, tree-filled darkness seemed to be full of presences: whispers, murmurings, a snapped twig beneath a ghostly foot, a sudden breath of air against the cheek, as though someone—something—invisible had hurried by.

"Spooky," whispered Rush, and laughed softly to hide the fact that he felt shivery.

"Is it? Guess 'tis. I've been in these woods so much I know 'em like my own backyard and like 'em a lot better."

They stole on. Branches snapped in Rush's face, moths whirred past his ears, and he got a mouthful of cobwebs. Far away he heard the soft, strange voices of owls.

"*What's that?*" he cried suddenly, stopping dead in his tracks and grabbing hold of Mark.

Ahead of them something stood unmoving in their path: something large and low that glowed with a cold, unearthly light. Rush was certain that he saw a ghost at last; he could actually feel the hair rising on his head.

But Mark was laughing.

"That's fox fire," he said. "It's only a dead stump. Sometimes dead wood gets like that when it's damp: phosphorescent. See." He chipped off a piece of the rotten wood and held it up. "It keeps on shining when you touch it."

Rush held the piece in the palm of his hand: a little witch light with no warmth.

"I've seen phosphorus in the ocean on a summer night," he said. "Tiny points of light like stars all along the waterline, but I never knew about this. Randy'd like it."

"We'll show her sometime. Keep quiet now, we're not far off. You'll have to keep *awful* quiet. They'd skin us alive if they caught us."

Rush felt a delicious mingling of fear and curiosity: one part fear to three parts curiosity. He crouched like an Indian, stepped on tiptoe, hardly breathed as he walked.

In a few minutes they could smell smoke, and heard voices, a man laughing.

"Easy now," whispered Mark, putting a restraining hand on Rush's arm.

Inch by inch they crept forward. There was a light somewhere spraying out through the leaves: the shifty, uncertain light of a fire in the open. Smoke bit into their nostrils.

Rush caught his foot on a dead branch and stumbled with a crash.

The two boys froze. They were so still that they could hear their own heartbeats, and the dark seemed to prickle with a thousand tiny lights.

After a long second Mark let go of his breath in a sigh. "They didn't notice. Lie down on the ground."

Cautiously they let themselves down until they were stretched flat on their stomachs.

"Kind of inch forward like a caterpillar," Mark said. "Follow me."

Little by little they made their way toward the light. It was scratchy and uncomfortable. Leaves got into Rush's eyes, nose, and mouth. He kept spitting out spiders, webs, twigs, and other foreign bodies. His stomach was scratched unmercifully and he put one hand down on a decayed, wet toadstool with a shudder of horror.

Soon he was aware that Mark had stopped crawling, was lying still just ahead of him; and that the lights and voices were now very close. Inch by inch Rush crawled up beside him.

He saw that they were lying at the edge of a little bluff looking down into a pocket (perhaps another abandoned quarry) in the hillside. Somewhere there was a tinkle of running water. The boys were so close to the occupants of the hollow that the screen of beech leaves and ferns that protected them seemed very frail security to Rush.

"What are they doing? What is that thing?" he breathed into Mark's ear.

"It's a still," Mark breathed back. "You know, for making stuff to drink. Corn whisky they make. It's against the law."

"Why do they make it, then? Why don't they buy it if they want it?"

"This doesn't cost anything; not even the price of a license. That's why."

Down in the hollow a fire was burning beneath a strange-looking object. It seemed to be a round turnip-shaped container with a metal coil coming out of the top of it. The coil was attached to a large hogshead. Around this contraption the men were grouped. Five, Rush counted. Two were sitting on a log, two on the ground. Oren was standing by the still, the firelight shining on his narrow face. Besides himself there were two large, shaggy men with full beards and longish hair. There was a tall weedy man with no chin, and a great fat one with a white round face like a Stilton cheese. The men were passing a gallon vinegar jug from one to the other. But from the relish with which each of them tilted it up and drank from it, it was obvious that the jug no longer contained vinegar.

"Who are the ones with beards?" whispered Rush.

"The Delacey brothers, Cedric and Fitzroy. They live up back a ways, right in the woods where it's hard to get to. They have a cabin there, and they fish, and hunt, and set traps, and live like a couple of bears. They never come down to Carthage even, only about twice a year—"

"Trying to forget their names I bet," Rush said. "And who's the fat one?"

"That's Mr. Waldemar Crown. He's a real educated man, but he's bad. Even Oren says so. He's s'posed to have murdered a man a long time ago, but they couldn't ever prove it. And when the Carthage bank was robbed five years ago they thought he was the one behind it. But they never could prove that either. Everyone's scared of him except Oren and the Delaceys. He never can keep hired help on his place."

Rush felt distinctly creepy. This was the first really bad person he had ever seen. Even Oren wasn't a criminal.

"Who's the tall thin one?"

"Johnny Cortain. He mows lawns and does odd jobs around. He's kind of weak in the head, but they say when they get in a jam down to the bank they call in Johnny. Anything to do with numbers is duck soup to him, he's better than an adding machine. There's no harm in Johnny, he's just kind of weak and silly."

"Quite a bunch," said Rush. "I wish Cuffy could see me now."

The fat man, Waldemar Crown, had apparently just told a joke, for suddenly the men began to laugh. The two with the beards kept hitting their knees and howling. Great bear howls came out of their shaggy mouths.

Johnny Cortain had a high-pitched giggle, and even Oren's narrow mouth turned up at one corner.

"Well, it's an old joke," said the fat man, "but I daresay it's new to you. After all, you don't get about very much do you, any of you? At least not in the realm of light entertainment. It would be rather unrewarding for the Delacey boys to swap anecdotes with the company *they* keep: woodchucks, and skunks, and squirrels. Johnny never remembers a story, and you, Oren, confine your social life to the livestock on your farm. You ought to go about more."

"Well, I'm gointa!" said Oren unexpectedly, setting down the vinegar jug, with which he had been refreshing himself at some length. "I'm gointa clear out. Gointa sell the farm. I've had enough of it. Fed up and through. I won't git much for it, but I'll git enough to lift me out of here. Then I'll clear out. Git me one of these defense jobs that pays good, or set up with a fella I know on a fruit ranch in California."

"Whatcha going to do with the kid?" said Johnny Cortain. "Take him along?"

"N-a-a. Take him along! He ain't nothin' but a weight around my neck. I'm aimin' to let the county look after him if he can't look after himself. Them Welfare people been nosin' around too much. Now they'll git him for good, let them worry about him for good!"

Rush put his hand on Mark's shoulder. "Gee," he said.

"The authorities may have something to say about

that," declaimed the fat man, who for unpleasant reasons of his own was an authority on the authorities. "I wonder if they'll let you step out so easily."

Oren smiled his crooked smile. "Ever hear of a fella changin' his name? I got one all picked, and what's more I got an advantage in my face. It don't show up good in a crowd; there's a lot of folks looks like me—"

"And they ain't the kind of folks anyone cares to look at twice," observed a Delacey brother, pawing the air in mirth while Oren scowled.

"It's an inconspicuous type, granted," said the fat man. "Well, more power to you, Oren. I'm a great believer in the individual liberties myself."

"And how!" agreed the other Delacey. The fat man ignored him.

"Now what I have in mind is this," he said. "Your boy—what is his name?"

"Mark Herron. And he ain't *my* boy."

"Yes, Mark. I myself could use a lively boy about the place. I can't keep any hired help longer than a week or so, but a boy like that, young, dependent . . . it would dispense with the question of salary, and a charitable act on my part, just at this moment, would be both becoming and salutary."

"It's okay with me," said Oren indifferently, and stooped down again for the jug.

Rush looked at Mark. His eyes were glittering in the firelight, showing grief or rage, or both.

"Doggone him! He won't do it, I won't let him. I'll run away first," whispered Mark savagely.

"Darn right you won't. You come live with us, that's what you do."

"Your father would like that fine, I bet. Thanks just the same though. I'm glad we came here tonight. I thought Oren was acting queer."

One of the Delacey brothers lifted his large nose.

"I smell a dang funny smell. You know what it is, Fitzroy?"

Fitzroy also lifted his nose.

"You two have noses like wild animals," said the fat man. "Have another drink."

"I smell it too," cried Johnny Cortain in his reedy voice. "It's citronella, that's what it is. It's to keep mosquitoes away. Who's got it on? I ain't."

"Just as soon wear perfumery," grunted a Delacey. "It's you, ain't it, Crown?"

The fat man shook his head.

"They don't bite me; I imagine I have a bitter rind like a lemon."

" 'Tain't Oren, neither, it's comin' downwind," said the first Delacey, lumbering to his feet. "Strong enough to knock you over. Bring the lantern, Fitzroy."

Before Rush scrambled away from the bluff edge he saw that the Delacey had a shotgun in his hand.

"Quick!" whispered Mark.

Their headlong flight was noisy and terrifying. Like

frightened stags they crashed through the underbrush. Behind them there was more crashing, loud bellows, and a few wild shots from the gun. But before long the hullabaloo ceased and Mark slowed down.

"Jeepers!" said Rush. "Jeepers W. Creepers! I never was shot at before in my whole life. Jeepers."

"Oh, they prob'ly just shot it off up in the air to scare us," Mark said. "But I'm glad they couldn't see us."

"All I need is a ten-gallon hat and a good horse," said Rush. "Hi-ho, Silver. Jiminy, I never thought I'd go through anything like that. What would they have done if they'd caught us?"

"Let's not try to guess. They don't know it was us. They'd *never* guess you, because they don't know I know you, and Oren thinks I don't know about the still either; only when we get down to the creek I'm going to wash. If he ever smells citronella on me—"

"What will you do? About what he said, I mean?"

"I dunno. But I won't be kept by the county and I won't work for Crown. Do you think I could pass for eighteen?"

Rush almost laughed. "We-e-ll. No, I guess not."

"I wisht I could. I'd join the Marines."

"Be your age, Mark. You'll have to be anyway—you're thirteen. But don't you worry. When my father gets back from Washington I'll ask him. He knows a lot about everything."

Mark sighed. "I wisht I knew when Oren's planning to leave."

The creek was dark and cool-sounding, but Rush was too lazy and exhausted to bathe in it. He lay on the bank in a bed of mint, breathing in deep breaths, letting the night, and the fragrance, and the fresh sound of water wash away the ugliness of what he had seen and heard. Mark scrubbed and splashed near-by but he wasn't enjoying it. He was worrying.

"Gee, I wisht I knew what to do."

"It'll be okay," said Rush. He felt sorry for Mark, but he knew his father would think of something. "I'll write to him if he doesn't come soon," he said.

He was half asleep by the time Mark had come out of the creek and dressed himself.

"I don't see how I could smell of citronella now," said Mark. "I even washed my hair!" A few seconds later he said, "A mosquito just bit me, so it's all right. Gee, I never thought I'd be glad to have a mosquito bite me."

The repercussions of that night were several. Rush got home so late that Cuffy scolded him straight into bed. She even opened his door after the light was out to tell him an extra thing or two about his behavior.

Isaac arrived still later, and by daylight it was apparent to everyone that he had had an argument with a skunk, and that the skunk had had the ultimate triumphant word.

"Keep hib *oud* of here. Keep hib oud!" cried Mona frantically, holding her nose. "What a *dawful* sbell! Revoltig!"

It was Rush's sad duty to purify Isaac. He did it with the

garden hose, brown soap, white soap, a scrubbing brush, and a bottle of eau de Cologne (Mona's). It took all morning, and at the end of it Cuffy swore all that had happened was that Rush had transferred the smell to his own person. He was handed his luncheon through the kitchen window and made to eat it out of doors. After that he himself had a bath with the hose. Nobody would let him use the pool.

That night Rush woke up feeling as though there were crumbs under his skin, and by the next morning he had developed a howling case of poison ivy. He wondered if Mark had it too, but wistfully decided that he probably hadn't, that the bath in the creek had undoubtedly saved him.

"What I can't understand," said Cuffy, scrubbing him raw with a nailbrush and brown soap, "is why it's broke out all over your front like that."

But Rush, remembering that brief unpleasant journey on his stomach through the dark woods, understood all too clearly, and sighed the deep, patient sigh of a martyr bound by secrecy.

CHAPTER VII

The Twelve-Pound Cat

"Best worms is down by the old pigsty," said Mr. Titus, ambling off in that direction. "Rich earth there. Real rich. Worms love it; night crawlers. I've hooked many a good-size bluegill on a night crawler. Yes, and better than bluegills, too."

He detached one of his apron strings from the reaching tendrils of a morning-glory vine.

"They can talk about their plugs for casting all they wanta, and their feather flies and spoons, and I don't know what all. Let 'em talk, I say, but give me good live bait. Yessir," said Mr. Titus rolling the words around in his mouth like a fat giant in a fairy tale. "Give me good LIVE BAIT!"

Oliver, plowing along behind him, agreed heartily.

He agreed with everything Mr. Titus did or said. As a fisherman, storyteller, baker of cakes, and general all-round person, Oliver found Mr. Titus without fault. Ever since Rush had allowed him to accompany them on a fishing trip Oliver had taken every opportunity to see Mr. Titus. He had even bought a straw hat at the Carthage Dry Goods and Confectionery exactly like Mr. Titus's. It had a green celluloid skylight set into the front brim that cast a bilious light upon his face. The only trouble was that it had looked too new, and Oliver was aging it by stepping on it now and then, rolling it in the dust, and picking at the edge of the brim to make it ravel. He had done a pretty good job on it in a short time, and the hat looked almost as experienced as that of his idol.

Mr. Titus encouraged this friendship. He fostered it tenderly with rich night crawlers, and marble cake, and all-day excursions to Abbot's Slough, or Squaw Dam, or one of the many little ponds or streams that he knew about.

"There's the place, right about there." Mr. Titus indicated a spot in the dark, pigpen soil with the toe of his shoe. "Here's the trowel, Oliver. I'm too old and fat to have to bend down. You dig 'em out and I'll point 'em out. I'm an expert worm-diviner."

What he said was true. In very little time they had a Mason jar full of good, active live bait.

Next they picked up the lunch basket (an important item), and with their fishing rods and identical straw hats walked side by side along the dusty road toward the slough that ran through Bagget's pasture. Oliver was even beginning to walk a little like Mr. Titus. Hambone wagged along beside them.

On either side the ragweed stood five feet tall and in lavish bloom.

"Bad for folks with hay fever," remarked Mr. Titus. "My sister's husband gets it something fierce. Claims the only cure he knows of is to go to some big city like New York City and ride back and forth all day long on the subway cars. And even then he ain't safe. Why, he says more folks travel around with bokays of flowers than you'd ever figure on. Oughta be a law, he says. Now then, let's see. You scooch down under this fence, Oliver, and I'll just step *over*; that's it. And down yonder under that old willow we oughta find a pool with some bluegills in it."

The next few hours were a time of peace and profit to them both. The willow lay along the bank like a scaly old dragon and arched its silver branches above the pool. It was ancient and vast, with great dead patches in it: decayed boughs and atrophied root stumps clawed the air, where the leathery fungus stood out in porte-cochères, and dark moss grew like ragged fur. But the rest of the tree was victoriously alive; supple, enormous, with thousands of leaves that moved softly and richly in the slightest wind.

"Sure is an old one," said Mr. Titus. "Looked just 'bout the same time I was a kid. My initials is carved on it somewheres."

Hambone had gone exploring by himself. From time to time they heard a muffled bark and a scuffle in the distance. Mr. Titus laughed comfortably.

"A great hunter, Hambone is. Goes at it just as hearty as if he ever bagged anything. Every woodchuck for miles around is familiar with that dog. 'There comes Hambone,' they tell each other. '*He* ain't anything to worry about. Just relax, boys, and we'll have a little fun.' Nice thing about it is Hambone don't know the joke's on him."

There was silence again. On the butterscotch-colored surface of the pool whirligig beetles and waterskaters went about their tiny, frantic business. The frogs came out one by one, and sat on the bank staring at nothing, their eyes glazed with gold and their front toes turned in.

Mr. Titus and Oliver sat side by side in the green shadow, holding their rods on their knees, staring out watchfully from under their twin hats. Both of them smelled strongly of citronella, and each approaching mosquito departed immediately with a frustrated whine. Above the citronella there was an odor of crushed mint, and slow water, and cow pastures. Every now and then, up- or downstream, something plopped into the slough: maybe a turtle, maybe a big frog. Maybe a snake. The dragonflies hung above the still surface like turquoise needles and woodpeckers knocked at the dead willow branches up above. The opposite bank was a rich jungle of jewelweed and boneset.

Mr. Titus sighed.

"I ever tell you about the time I caught the cat?"

"No, you never did," said Oliver, in anticipation. He was such a veteran, by now, that he knew immediately that Mr. Titus was referring not to an animal but to a fish. "Tell me."

"Well, it was like this. One day, two, three hundred years ago, when I was about's old as you, or maybe a little older, I went fishin' on a Sunday. Yessir, I went fishin' on a Sunday, and what's more, I played hooky from church to do it. That was a mighty sinful thing in those days. Guess 'tis still. Trouble was in Sunday school we'd been studyin' about Jonah and how 'the Lord had prepared a great fish to swallow up Jonah,' and how he was in its belly three days and three nights. Well, the more I got to thinkin' about that whale, that big fish of the Lord, the more I got to thinkin' about the big catfish that'd been layin' around a certain pool I knew of down to Abbot's Slough. I thought about it and thought about it till I couldn't stand it anymore, and then when class was over I lighted out quick's a wink before my folks could find me and take me to the church service. The buggies was all lined up in front, horses tied to the hitchin' rail, the bell was dingdongin' in the steeple, and I saw the ladies going in in their best dresses and their best religious smiles, and I hid for a while behind the horse trough until— Oop, wait, I got a bite!"

Excitedly Mr. Titus reeled in a small sheepshead, and removed it from the hook.

"I'll have it for breakfast tomorra," he said with satisfaction. "Rolled in corn meal, with bacon, and a pan of biscuit and some coffee. Let's see, where was I?"

"Behind the horse trough," prompted Oliver.

"That's right. Well, I just stayed there till I heard the organ begin (first it always gave kind of a grunt and a die-away sigh, and then even right through the music you could hear the sound of the foot pedals, thump-thump, thump-thump, just like someone goin' upstairs). And then when I heard the people singin' good and loud I started to run. Right across the meadows in my Sunday shoes that squeezed something terrible, because I was used to goin' barefoot. While I ran I could hear the singin' stop and then people coughin' for a minute and then the preacher, Mr. Kornhauser (he had a good strong voice), began the sermon. Callin' out loud from the pulpit, 'Remember the Sabbath day, to keep it holy'—I felt like he was callin' me sure, but I kept on runnin'. When I got home I sneaked right out back of the barn to get my tackle and bait. I didn't dare go near the house because my aunt Effie and my grandma was there gettin' dinner ready. They was makin' somethin' kinda fancy out of it because the preacher himself was comin' back for dinner. Even the thought of that didn't stop me in my sin. No, sir, I went right on down, right through the pasture to Abbot's Slough, near where it opens into the river, and all the time I had a feelin' I was gointa catch that fish. It was what they call a hunch, I guess.

"Well, I was so excited I didn't even take off my Sunday shoes and go barefoot. I went up near the mouth of the slough where that deep muddy pool was, and I stood there in the shade in my good suit and my good shoes, and I put the juiciest night crawler on my hook. Then I cast it out and waited. I swear my heart was right up in my throat; I just *knew* I was gointa get that cat.

"The old fat rascal was layin' around there on the bottom lookin' for a meal. I couldn't see him but I knew he was there. The little frogs sat around on the edge and blinked their yellow eyes, and bulged out their throats. None of them knew it was Sunday. The little birds, redwing blackbirds and woodpeckers, they was busy up in the branches flyin' around, and peckin', and hollerin' at each other. *They* didn't know it was Sunday. Neither did the mosquitoes.

"I kept tellin' myself that Sunday was just another day of the week and finally I had myself believin' it. All except my conscience. My conscience sat off on the side somewheres, knowin' it was Sunday and judgin' me. But I managed to keep it from comin' too close.

"It was a fine morning, clear and bright. Hot in the sunshine and cool in the shade, and locusts made that scorching noise up in the trees. I stood there maybe an hour, maybe two, and I didn't catch a thing except some duckweed and cress. I was beginnin' to get hungry, and the hungrier I got the closer came my conscience. 'You should of thought sooner,' it was sayin'. 'You'd oughta know they won't give you any dinner *now*. Not after you skippin' church.'

"And then, by golly, it happened! Something hit my line like an express train. I was so dumbfounded that I lost my balance and I didn't have no toes to grip with as they were all closed up in those blame shoes. Down I went, flat's a haddock and slid right into the pool. It's a deep one there, or used to be. Maybe ten, twelve foot. I went down with my eyes open and under the water it was yellow like chicken broth. All the time I was holdin' onto my rod, too. I hadn't learnt to swim yet, but when I came to the surface I wanted to get back to the bank so bad that, by golly, I got there! Don't ask me how.

"And all the time I was hangin' onto my rod for dear life; and when I scrambled up the muddy bank and pulled myself onto the grass I kept sayin' to my conscience (or maybe it was a prayer), 'Just let that fish be on my line still. Just let him be hooked good, and I'll promise never to fish on Sunday again long as I live. Honest to goodness cross my heart.'

"Well, sir, the fish *was* on. He was on and I sure had a tussle gettin' him in. But I got him in! Yessir, I got him in.

And he was a beauty, too. Fat and independent, with whiskers like a Chinese emperor; the biggest cat I'd ever seen. I felt like I'd won a battle single-handed. I felt like I deserved a medal.

"He weighed a plenty, that fish did. He weighed twelve pounds and a little over, the biggest catfish ever caught in Abbot's Slough. I carried him along and I didn't care how heavy he was. The water in my shoes squelched with every step, the knees was out of both my stockin's and my lace collar was full of watercress, but I didn't care. At least at first I didn't. Then when I climbed the fence and began crossing Volkmann's pasture my clothes commenced to steam; the sun got hotter and hotter, and the fish got heavier and so did my conscience. I walked slower and slower. I wished I didn't ever have to go home.

"I saw the house and the maple trees around it, and the barn all quiet in the noonday sunshine, and *they* knew it was Sunday all right. So did our dog, Shep, on the front steps, and so did all the Leghorn hens. They was standin' around the barnyard white as snow, makin' little thin sounds and not movin' much. Everything sat there neat and tidy in the sunshine, knowin' it was Sunday and condemnin' me.

"Well, by the time I came through the side gate I was plannin' how I'd hide in the hayloft till it was dark and then get into the house, change my clothes, open my bank and run away to join the Wild West show.

"But my grandma saw me out the kitchen window. She had an eye like a chicken hawk.

"'JASPER!' she hollers. Big, like she was callin' a station on a train. 'JASPER!'

"I stopped in my tracks, drippin'.

"'You march straight into the parlor, young man, and see what your papa has to say to you!'

"And Aunt Effie (I never did care for her) kept sayin', 'My heavenly day! My *Lands*! Why, Jasper Titus, and on a Sunday, and with Mr. Kornhauser here, too! Just look at your suit, and your lovely croshay collar! I just hope your papa whips you!'

"And my sister Ruthie. She was no help. She just stared at me and kind of held her skirts away and said, 'My, 'm I ever glad it's not *me*!'

"Nobody mentioned the fish.

"I squelched into the parlor to meet my doom.

"There they was sittin', full of Sunday dinner and wholesome satisfaction because they'd worshiped first and then et. And there I stood in the doorway, mud from top to toe, and with my stockin's tore, but holdin' the biggest cat that ever come out of Abbot's Slough.

"They all just stared at me. My mamma in her best silk dress. Mrs. Kornhauser in *her* best silk dress. My papa in his stiff collar, and watch chain looped across his stummick, and Mr. Kornhauser. Mr. Kornhauser's mouth fell open like the mouth on a carp.

"'Jasper, what happened to you, are you hurt?' says my mamma. 'We was callin' you and callin' you—'

"'Hurt, indeed!' says my papa, pushin' back his chair. 'He played hooky, that's what he done. Hooky! On a Sunday! From church!'

"'But, Gilbert, he's soakin' wet,' says my mamma.

"'How did you get wet, young man? Answer me!' shouts my papa. 'What's that you got there?'

"'A fish, papa,' I says. My voice sounds weak.

"I held up the fish and I couldn't help but be glad that it was so big. If I'd done an awful wicked thing by playin' hooky on Sunday I was glad anyways that the result was a fine big catfish instead of a measly little perch. It was on a nobler scale. (And I don't mean a fish scale either, heh-heh. That's what they call a pun.)

"'Oh, Jasper, *fishin'*!' my mamma says, lookin' real sad. She didn't know much about fish. But just for a second I saw my papa staring at that cat with his eyes bungin' out, and he didn't look mad a bit.

"'Jasper,' says Mr. Kornhauser, and that big voice of his booms out just like he'd brought his pulpit with him. 'Jasper, you have forgotten, I fear—"And on the seventh day thou shalt rest . . ."'

"I wanted to say that fishin' was restin' to me and church was work, but I had the sense not to. My papa was lookin' mad again and I knew what was in store for me. A whippin' behind the barn with all the hens scurryin' away and squawkin' and then being sent to my room with no dinner, and then a long talk with Mamma.

"That's what I got, too. And I repented like I should have done, and the hungrier I got the more I repented. Finally I thought I'd repented about as much as the sin was worth, and I opened my bedroom window and looked out. My sister Ruthie was in the double swing with her dolls. I waved a towel (I didn't dare call) till she noticed it. She came skippin' over.

"'I'm hungry,' I says.

"'Wait a minute,' she says, and ran into the house.

"Pretty soon she came back with a basket, and I let down a rope I kept behind the washstand (that wasn't the first time I'd been sent to my room). Ruthie tied on the basket and I pulled it up. I remember's if it was yesterday: chicken leg and cold turnips and a slice of pie. Ruthie was a good sister."

Mr. Titus lapsed into silence. Oliver waited a minute and then said, "Is that the end of the story, Mr. Titus?"

"Pretty close to it, Oliver, but not quite.

"Well, sir, a long time later, when I was near grown, my papa died. Some days after the funeral Mamma and Ruthie and I went through his things, his papers and all, you know. Papa always used to keep a journal, mostly about crops, like how many bags of feed he'd bought and how much they'd cost, or how much he'd got for the Chester sow he'd sold, and things like that. I was just flippin' the pages through my fingers, lookin' at the entries without payin' much attention when I saw one that caught my eye.

"'Sunday, August 8, 1886,' it read. 'Today my son Jasper Joseph Titus caught a 12-pound catfish. Probably the largest ever caught in Abbot's Slough.'"

Oliver thought this over.

"So he wasn't mad, after all," he said at last.

"So he wasn't mad, after all," agreed Mr. Titus. "I was kinda glad to know about it." Then he laughed a little. "But that sure was a mighty convincin' spankin' he gave me behind the barn."

By the time he had caught another sheephead and Oliver had caught two bluegills it was time for supper. Mr. Titus's basket always contained surprises and Oliver watched its unpacking with appreciative attention. At the appearance of each item he said, "Boy!" or "Oh, boy!" with enthusiasm. Deviled eggs, oh, boy. *Boy*, minced chicken sandwiches! Orange layer cake, oh, boy, oh, boy, oh, boy!

"Yes, and root beer," said Mr. Titus.

After they had eaten every crumb they fished some more. Minnows began jumping in the still water. The shadows deepened. There was a sound of cows returning to their barns.

"Time to go, Oliver, time to go," said Mr. Titus, getting up from the ground in sections. "We done pretty good today. Next time we'll do better. Now, where's that dog of mine? *Hambone!* Here, sir, come here."

Hambone appeared almost at once, bounding eagerly,

his coat full of sticktights and one of his ears turned inside out.

"It's a good thing Hambone ain't a fisherman," said Mr. Titus as they crossed the pasture. "He'd be awful unlucky."

They negotiated the fence once more, and side by side walked up the dusty road, in shadow now. Mr. Titus's walk was a little stiffer than at midday, and Oliver's was a little slower. But they had their fish and their empty picnic basket and they were well content.

Several times they passed long lines of cows going home to be milked. They were soft-colored animals, and the dust rose in clouds about their hoofs. Great velvety melancholy sounds came from their throats. With each herd there was a little boy in overalls. Each time they said, "Hello," and the boy said, "H'lo, catch any?" And they held up their fish for him to see.

An evening fragrance came from the woods and ditches. The sky was deepening up at the top.

"Gee, Mr. Titus," Oliver said. "My, I wish *I* could ever catch a twelve-pound cat."

"You will, son, you will. And bigger, too," said Mr. Titus generously. After a moment he added, "But not in Abbot's Slough."

CHAPTER VIII

A Noise in the Night

Cuffy had a cousin, a widow, named Mrs. Theobald. The Melendy children had never seen her but they knew about her. They knew that her first name was Coral, that she lived in Ithaca, N. Y., was very fat, had two little old white poodles, couldn't stand the heat, had fallen arches, and knew how to make the richest fruitcake in the United States.

One day Mrs. Theobald sneezed as she was going downstairs, lost her footing, fell and broke three ribs. The doctor and the neighbors begged her to go to a hospital. But no, she would not go and leave her poodles to the care of another.

"My cousin, Mrs. Evangeline Cuthbert-Stanley, will be delighted to look after me for a week or two," declared Mrs. Theobald. "I will telegraph her."

Mrs. Evangeline Cuthbert-Stanley, believe it or not, was Cuffy's real name, and when the telegram came she was far from delighted.

"Why, I can't just go and leave you children by yourselves," she clucked. "Here Mr. Melendy's down in Washington for the Lord knows how long."

"Willy's here," Mona said. "He wouldn't let anything happen to us. And there are the dogs, and after all I'm past fifteen."

"It's not anything *happening* to you that I'm worried about," sniffed Cuffy. "I'm only thinking of the state the house'll get into with me gone. Rush will step out of his clothes every night, leave them on the floor, and step into clean ones every morning till they're all gone and he has to go without any. Randy will leave paint water around in glasses till they make rings on the furniture, or someone drinks one of 'em by accident and dies of paint poisoning. Mona will forget to make her bed day in and day out till I get home. She'll get talcum powder into the rug, and her shoes will collect all over the house. She's always taking them off and going barefoot nowadays. Shoes on the mantelpiece, windowsill, piano, everywhere. I know her. And *nobody* will wash the dishes!"

"What will Oliver do?" asked Randy, who was listening with grave interest.

"Oh, Oliver. Well, if you were all like *Oliver*! He's just as tidy as a little cat, aren't you, my lamb? Picked up his toys good as gold, ever since he was a baby. But I know what he will do, though. He'll disappear at bedtime meek and quiet as can be. Just disappear. And you'll never be able to track him down till he's good and ready, hours later. Next morning he'll have circles under his eyes from lack of sleep—oh, no, I can't leave you alone—"

"Yes, you can, Cuffy, yes, you can," they told her. "On our honor, we'll be tidier than we ever were before. We'll make Oliver go to bed at half past seven if we have to tie him in."

Almost persuaded but still reluctant, Cuffy went to pack her suitcase, and Rush, before she could relent, flew to the telephone to send her wire to Mrs. Theobald. He loved Cuffy, they all did, but wouldn't it be delicious to savor absolute freedom from authority for a while?

"But what about food?" moaned Cuffy suddenly, sitting down on her bed, with her best shoes in her hands. "Oh, I can't go. Left to yourselves you'll eat nothing but liverwurst and baloney, and jelly sandwiches and bought doughnuts and cheese. Oh, no, I can't—"

"Cuffy," said Mona, taking a shoe out of Cuffy's hand and putting it firmly on her foot. "We will drink a gallon of milk a day. We'll eat carrots for breakfast. We'll eat spinach and oatmeal till it comes out of our ears.

We'll be good as angels. We honestly, honestly will!"

"Well, all right," said Cuffy unhappily. "But if Coral Theobald had any sense she'd of chloroformed them blame poodles long ago. Don't see how she broke her ribs anyway. All padded in fat like that—"

"Now, Cuffy, be charitable. You know you like her, she's a very fine woman," said Rush, sitting on her suitcase and snapping it shut with a click of finality. "This will be a nice vacation for you."

"Vacation, my eye," retorted Cuffy, banging on her hat as though she were slapping the lid onto a kettle. "You don't know Coral, poor soul. And you don't know them poodles. But I'll be back before the week is up, you mark my words."

Willy had harnessed Lorna Doone to the surrey and driven around to the front door. Rush carried Cuffy's suitcase, Randy her handbag (her satchel, Cuffy called it), and Mona had her coat. Oliver brought up the rear with three graham crackers and a slice of cake done up in a piece of paper towel, because "She might get hungry on the train." It was his own idea.

"Don't forget to keep the screen doors closed," commanded Cuffy, one foot on the carriage step. "If it storms don't forget to put a pan under that leak in the Office. Mona, you remember to give Oliver his vitamin B, and, Rush, you're to lock all the doors every single night! Don't change the beds till Friday. The doctor's telephone number is hanging by the hall phone. Oh, dear, there's so many things that I don't think I ought—" Cuffy took her foot down from the step.

But between them Rush and Mona simply boosted her into the surrey.

"We'll be *all right,*" they assured her. "You go on and don't worry. Make your cousin Coral give you a fruitcake to bring home."

Still looking anxious and rebellious, Cuffy was driven away from her brood.

"Go to bed on time!" they heard her calling from far down the drive. "Call me long-distance if anything goes wrong. Don't forget to feed the *dogs*!"

As if any of them would forget that!

They went back into the house feeling reckless and independent. Rush went galloping up the stairs three at a time, and in a few minutes they could hear him banging out the Revolutionary Etude fortissimo, with the sustaining pedal down. What a noise! Mona took her shoes off and put them on the hall table.

"I think I'll make a pie," she said, stretching her bare toes luxuriously. She walked over to the mirror and began fussing with her hair. "And I think I'll wear my hair up all the time Cuffy's gone."

"Okay, and I'll do a portrait of you," said Randy. "I'll make it big this time, life size almost. I'll make you wearing a long dress and jewelry, and I'll call it 'Reverie,' or 'Youth,' or something like that." All the time she was talking Randy was moving the living-room furniture.

Pushing tables and chairs against the wall, and rolling up small rugs.

"What are you doing, for heaven's sake?"

"Making more space. I want to practice my arabesques here where I can look in the mirror. Cuffy never lets me."

"Oh. Well, I don't see why not. As long as you move it all back again."

As for Oliver, he was busily sliding down the banisters over and over again. Cuffy didn't like him to because there was no newel post at the bottom, and she was always afraid he would fly off the end and crack his spine. Oliver knew he never would, but was kind enough to humor her. However, now that she was gone it seemed too good a chance to waste. Down he went, wind whistling in his ears, stopping just short of the end, and then up he went again, one sturdy foot after the other. He was singing to himself. He sang two lines of a song.

> *"Praise the Lord and pass the ammunition,*
> *And we'll all stay free-ee."*

These two lines he sang over and over, without amplification and without much tune, but he enjoyed it, and while he was singing and climbing upstairs he was planning not to weed his garden at all until the day before Cuffy came back. He was planning not to take any baths until the night before she came back. He was planning to fish all day, taking his lunch with him, and no nonsense about resting afterward.

> *"Praise the Lord and pass the ammunition,*
> *And we'll all stay FREE!"*

Mona's pie was a terrible failure. Randy found her almost in tears over the dough.

"Every time I try to roll it out the darn stuff just follows the rolling pin and curls up around it like a snake. I can't make it lie down!"

"Cuffy puts flour on the rolling pin." Randy, hot and panting from a half hour of arabesques, sank into a kitchen chair.

"Oh." There was silence for a minute.

"But now look at it, will you. It won't stretch. It just goes into holes."

"Put it on anyway, and maybe we can patch it."

By the time they'd patched it, the pie (lumpy with rhubarb) looked like a badly built igloo.

"But I bet it will taste delicious," said Randy warmly. And it probably would have, too, if Mona had remembered to put in the sugar.

Willy Sloper had supper with them. As a special treat they had it out on the lawn among the mosquitoes, because it was so hot; and Mona made iced coffee. "Just this once," she said. "I don't think Cuffy'd mind, do you?"

"Maybe she wouldn't," Randy agreed doubtfully. But Rush only winked at them over his glass, and prudently said nothing.

When they had tasted the pie, and each according to his manners and temperament repudiated it (Oliver leapt to his feet at the first bite as if he'd been stung, uttering howls of anguish), Willy saved the day by driving them all to Carthage in the surrey, and buying ice-cream cones. When they got back it was only half an hour after Oliver's bedtime, and he went to his room as docile as a lamb.

By nine o'clock it was so hot that Rush suggested a swim before they went to bed.

"We shouldn't," Mona said. "Cuffy wouldn't like it." But her tone had no conviction.

It was almost dark, and there were no stars. The sky glared suddenly with heat lightning, and there was a trembling of thunder in the air. Dead still it was, not a breath anywhere. They could hear a whippoorwill someplace in the woods.

"It sounds more like a machine than a bird," Rush said. "Sometimes it almost runs down when it's been going on for a long time. It begins stuttering: 'Whip-poor-will, whip-poor-will, whip-ip-ip-ip-oor-will, whip-ip-ip.'"

The water in the pool was warm. They basked in it up to their chins, like crocodiles. Mosquitoes whined along the surface and they splashed them away. It was too late in the summer for fireflies, but now and then a pale moth, almost luminous, hovered just above their heads.

Something, the iced coffee perhaps, or the heat, kept Rush awake for a long time that night; and even when he began to doze he had restless dreams. He kept seeing Oren Meeker, and the harsh faces of the men at the still. He imagined himself running through a midnight forest with these men in pursuit. Among the trees sat giant whippoorwills with phosphorescent eyes, and their calling was so loud that it was terrifying. Only what they were calling was, "Meeker's still! Meeker's still! Meeker's still!"

He kept running and running, more and more frightened, and then suddenly the woods split asunder and he was face to face with a terrible animal, a sort of fiery hippopotamus, and it was making a hideous, braying noise.

Rush opened his eyes. The dream vanished but the noise remained. He sat up in bed, heart knocking, and listened. It was, yes, of course—it was the Carthage fire siren.

Rush tumbled down the stairs to the telephone, hardly knowing what he was doing. He took down the receiver and waited for the night operator's sleepy question, "Number, please?"

"Hello, Miss Clisbee, where's the fire?" Rush said.

"Over to Meeker's farm."

"Meeker's! Is it bad?"

"Pretty bad, I guess. They've even sent for the outfit over to Eldred."

"Gee." Rush hung up. An instant later he picked up the

receiver again. "Thanks," he said into the mouthpiece.

Randy hated waking up before she was ready to. "Go '*way*!" she grumbled, as Rush shook her shoulder. "Leave me '*lone*!"

"Randy! Wake up! Meeker's farm's on fire!"

"Meeker's farm? Is it? How do you know?"

"Miss Clisbee told me. I'm going over, I want to see if Mark's okay. Don't let on to Mona if she wakes up."

"But I'm coming too!"

"No, sir, you're not. This isn't for girls."

"Yes, sir, I am." Randy leaped out of bed. "Mark's my friend just as much as yours."

"Well, then, hurry!" Rush gave up in exasperation. "I'll get our bikes out of the garage. I'm going to wake Willy up too."

Lucky it's hot, Randy was thinking. I don't have to waste much time on dressing. She stripped off her pajamas, put on her playsuit and sandals, and was ready to go. Down the stairs she flew on tiptoe. It was pitch-dark, but a light might waken Mona.

Outside the night was full of a strange clamor; braying fire siren, the windy bells of the engines, the rumbling thunder. The wind had sprung up while she was sleeping. It was vast and warm, and she felt that it was almost visible: a billowing, formless tide like clouds, or heavy smoke. She ran toward the garage, and bumped into Rush.

"Willy's not here," he whispered. "Left a light burning, and his radio on as usual."

"But where—?"

"To the fire probably. His bike's gone too. Here's yours. Does the headlight work? Good, so does mine. Let's get going."

It was spooky but exciting coasting along in the dark behind Rush. The warm, enormous wind fanned Randy's face and arms; the woods murmured like an ocean, and Randy did not dare to look at them. She knew how huge and powerful they became at night. Rush was too far ahead. She rang the bell on her handlebars to give herself courage, but instead it frightened her almost to death.

"What time is it, Rush?" she called tremulously.

"It's late. After one o'clock."

"Gosh," Randy said.

They left their bikes in the weeds where Meeker's road turned off; Rush's flashlight had gone dead, but they didn't need it after all. The sky was bright with the ominous light of fire. Now and then the lightning came: a flash of icy blue above the burning gold and crimson.

As they ran panting along the uneven ruts they stumbled and tripped. The tall weeds brushed against them, and reaching briars scratched their legs. Randy fell headlong over a root, and Rush pulled her up again before she had time to find out whether or not she was hurt. The road seemed endless. Rush felt as though he were still running in his nightmare.

Once there was a burst of light and noise behind them. Rush pulled Randy into the milkweed at the roadside.

The Eldred fire engine went snorting past them, all brass, bells, red paint, and lights. It left behind it a hot smell of gasoline, and a sudden quiet.

"Listen!" said Randy.

Her eyes opened wide with horror, for now they could hear the fire itself: a rich, jovial, mighty crackling.

"Oh, Mark! Oh, Mark! Oh, Mark!" moaned Randy, beginning to cry.

"Shut up, Ran, he'll be all right. You'll see." Rush was pale, all the same, and he began running faster yet.

Suddenly they came out of the woods; and stopped dead in their tracks.

The farmhouse was now a raging bonfire. Still through the flames they could see the shape of it, the dark hollows of its doors and windows with smoke and fire coming out. The flames drove upward from the walls and roof, high, high, in a great, dazzling, lifting mane. The voluminous smoke billowed higher still in genii shapes, red-brown against the blue-black sky, and shot through with flying sparks like fiery bees. Beside the house the dead pine was ablaze, every branch outlined in burning veins of light.

Down in the hollow stood the two fire engines and a handful of cars. Firemen were scurrying about untangling hoses, and from the well to the house stretched a long line of men and boys passing pails of water from hand to hand: a bucket brigade. On the outskirts stood the onlookers: small knots of women, old men, and children, their faces white in the firelight, their fascinated eyes glittering with reflected flames. Somebody had tied the two Meeker dogs to a fence, and there they stood barking incessantly, first one, then the other, then both together.

"Where's Mark? I don't see Mark," Randy kept saying.

"He's there someplace. Stop asking me that. He's bound to be someplace. Come on down and see."

They passed three old men and heard a snatch of conversation.

"Hope they don't pump the well dry with them hoses."

"Well, they say they got some kind of *chemical* to spray on too."

"Hope they have aplenty. Looks like it'd take more'n a Flit gunful."

"*There's* Mark!" cried Rush.

And there he was, coming out of the barn between the team of work horses, a hand on each bridle, light shining on his dazed face. Randy never forgot the way he looked then, so thin and small between the great bony horses.

"Oh, Mark, are you all right?" she cried, running up to him and forgetting the deep distrust she felt for all horses except Lorna Doone.

"Why, h'lo. Yes, I'm okay."

"Anything we can do, Mark?"

"I guess maybe you could help bring out the cows, Rush. They're afraid if the wind don't change the barn might catch."

"How did it start?"

"I dunno. I was asleep. The dogs woke me up barking,

then I smelt smoke and when I opened my door the stairs was on fire. I looked right into it like a furnace and then I closed the door, and next thing I knew I was out the window and halfway down that ol' dead pine, the one that's on fire now. It was a good ol' tree."

They all looked at the blazing tree.

"Then I heard someone calling my name. It was Herb Joyner; he saw the light from his bedroom window and came arunning in his pajamas right down the valley, and across the oat stubble in the back meadow. Barefoot, too—it must have hurt. He'd put in the call to Carthage before he left—"

"But—but Oren?"

"I dunno where he is. He went out right after milking. I hollered his name all the way down the tree . . . Guess he's still out." Mark looked at Rush. "*You* know. Sometimes he doesn't come home till morning."

"I'll start getting out the cows," Rush said.

"So will I," said Randy, and followed him into the barn.

The darkness smelled warm and healthy. It was full of deep, soft breathing and the rustle of hay. Randy stepped timidly up to the first cow. In the shadow it looked big as a mastodon, and its huge, still eyes stared at her out of its light face. Gee whiz, Randy thought, they say animals always know when you're scared of them. And I'm scared . . .

"Come on, bossy," she said aloud in a sweet, false voice.

The cow came out with a heavy dignified tread and sighed a great sigh that smelled of hay. Randy put up her hand and found the bridle. She stepped forward and the cow stepped with her, mild and docile. Randy felt love in her heart for the creature. Beautiful, trustful, obedient animal. I must tell Father we should have a cow, she said to herself, and to the cow she said, "Don't be frightened, don't be scared. We'd never let anything hurt you."

"Randy Melendy!" said an outraged voice. "What the dickens you doin' down here? I thought you was all safe asleep. What would your papa say?"

Randy looked up into Willy's indignant face; he was soaking wet and there was a bucket in his hand.

"I'm herding cattle," she said.

"Well, isn't that nice! I suppose you brought the whole family along, too?"

"No, just Rush."

"Oh, just Rush. And where is he, may I ask? Operatin' a hose or givin' the fire chief pointers, no doubt."

"Oh, now, Willy! Don't be mad, we'll be careful. Rush is herding cattle, too."

Soon all the cows were out. They stood at the edge of the pasture dazed in the brilliant light. Now and then one of them would comment on it in a great questioning voice.

The fire blazed higher than ever, high and arched, like a fiery sickle curved over the barn.

"'F they don't get both them pumps workin' soon they're gointa lose the barn sure. House is a goner already," said the watchers.

But now a stream, two streams, were directed at the flames. The bucket brigade, too, still did its work nobly, sweating, spilling great puddles of water, but never resting.

Nothing helped much. The fire had gone too far. It had burst its bonds like the undisciplined giant that it was, roaring, and chuckling, and reaching, hungry for everything in sight.

"Roof'l cave in soon now," someone said. "Better move back, sister, never can tell."

Randy stepped back in a daze, unable to look away from that dazzling spectacle.

"Where's Oren? Why the dickens don't he come home?" said a man. And another replied in a startled voice, "Gee whilikens, you don't suppose—! The kid said he was out all evenin'!"

"Naw, naw, he'd have smelled it sure."

Randy felt scared. She ran to find Rush or Willy or Mark.

Rush and Mark were getting the hogs out of the sty, and at the sight of those hideous, rumbling creatures, Randy did not offer to help.

"Step back all," commanded the fire chief suddenly. "Step back quick!"

And then there was a sound, a hollow, crashing, terrible sound. For an instant the flames swelled out sidewise, in a great mushroom of fire, and then curved upward again stronger than ever. The roof had caved in.

"Look, the barn's caught," yelled somebody, a woman, in a high, thin voice.

It was true. From the upper part of the barn the hay protruded: from the loft windows, and the door. It bulged out between the warped planks, squeezed through the cracks like oats sprouting through a rotten sack. Everywhere that the hay protruded little tongues of fire were licking.

"How fast it goes!" whispered Randy.

Mark was standing beside her, but he said nothing. He stood there staring at the destruction as though half asleep.

"Why don't the dang rain *rain*?" growled a bystander. "Look at it, will you, holdin' off just's long's it kin!"

After a long while the fires began to subside. A hundred other little fires seemed to leap and blaze in the puddles of water that had spilled from the buckets and leaked from the hoses. The Carthage firemen and the Eldred firemen worked like Trojans. They fought not only the fire but the wind, which, vast and dry, was in league with the fire, coaxing it on, fanning it high, carrying sparks toward the strawstacks, the dry meadows.

At four o'clock the battle was almost over but no one felt victorious, for the house was gone. Nothing remained of it but smoldering ashes and a charcoal skeleton. The barn fared little better, though it still carried the travesty of a roof.

The onlookers began to leave in tired groups. They felt let down, saddened at the outcome of the fire. There was a commotion of rattletrap cars; metal doors slammed, voices called, the Meeker dogs commenced to bark again. Above and beyond these sounds could be heard the tireless chopping and chopping of firemen's hatchets. Flashlights played about the wreckage.

The fire chief was talking to Willy Sloper and presently Willy came over to the children.

"Come on, kids," he said. "Show's over."

"But, Mark—" Randy said.

"Mark's comin' too. C'mon, Mark."

"Gee, thanks, but I can't. Oren wouldn't like to come home and find all this and me not here."

"You come on. I'll fix it with Oren. It's late. You know how late it is? Past four o'clock. Every rooster in the state will commence hollerin' in about ten minutes."

Mark argued no longer. Dog-tired, he followed Willy. Rush walked beside him, wide awake and full of thoughts; but Randy pitched and stumbled against him, suddenly half asleep. Rush put his arm through hers to guide her.

"My nose smells of smoke," Randy muttered.

"Your nose *smells* smoke, you mean."

"No, smells *of* it. I think it's going to forever. My hair too."

The whole valley had a scorched smell, in fact. Now and then there was a rift in the odor, and the large wind came through, carrying the undisturbed fragrance of night woods.

The lightning flared suddenly. For an instant Randy could see all things in sharp detail: Willy's old scuffed heels, the clover pressed flat in his footprint, the moth hovering over the wheel rut. Then darkness again and renewed thunder.

Also a drop of rain.

"There it comes," said Willy disgustedly. "Just missed the bus by a couple of hours. How do you like that!"

They were too weary even to resent it. By the time they came to the mailbox and picked up the bikes the rain was pelting down. They did not dare ride in all the wetness and confusion. Willy steered Randy's bike and Rush his own. They ran along the road, wet to the skin, slipping on loose stones, stumbling into ditches. Randy began to cry from strain and exhaustion, but nobody knew it. She swallowed her sobs quietly and the tears on her face might have been rain water. She would have died rather than let Rush know how she felt. "I told you so" is one of the horridest phrases in the English language.

"Mark can sleep in my room," Rush said.

"No, he can sleep in the cupola," Randy said. "That's the nicest place, and he once said he'd like to. And the bed's made up."

"Whatcha snifflin' about? Cold?" inquired Willy anxiously.

"I guess so."

"We'll be home in a jiffy. Better get right to bed, and take a hot-water bag with you."

"Listen to Grandmother Sloper," jeered Rush.

"I wish Cuffy was here," Randy said, with a gulp which she turned into a queer sounding sneeze.

"You and me both," agreed Willy unhappily.

Rush and Mark reached the driveway first. They walked with their heads bowed down against the rain and the bicycle between them.

"Do you think Oren was—at that place?"

"The still? Must've been. Sometimes he don't come home at all." Mark plowed on silently. Then Rush could see his pale face turned toward him. "What gets me is that he didn't hear the racket even up where he was."

"The wind was in the wrong direction, wasn't it?"

"Yes, that's right. Yes, it was. But even so—"

"Oh, well, don't worry about it. He'll know soon enough. Probably knows now."

That night Mark got his wish. He slept in the cupola. The rain beat on the little metal roof. It spattered against the four windows, and ran down in a long stream from the spout. The gutters tinkled and hummed. The thunder sounded as if it had been cut up in squares. It tumbled down the sky like giant blocks tumbling downstairs. Mark snarled himself into his favorite sleeping position and felt as if he had come home at last. The fire, the violence of the last few hours, the probable reactions of Oren, were thoughts too dreadful to contemplate now. A safety door in his brain locked itself against them, and soon he was asleep.

Mona couldn't understand why nobody but Oliver woke up the next morning. She had already started breakfast when Willy came in and told her what had happened.

"I think it's mean," complained Mona bitterly. "Somebody might have wakened me and Oliver. We like excitement too. And here the very *first* exciting thing all summer happens in the middle of the night and we sleep through it like—like hibernating bears!"

She was really very cross, and offered Willy a cup of cocoa as if she were offering him poison. He did look battered and smoke smudged and worn out, she noticed.

"Don't wake the kids up," Willy advised. "They had a hard night. I hope Mark sleeps all day. The poor kid's in for a shock, I'm afraid."

"Why?" said Mona, saucepan in mid-air. "Willy?"

"Oren never did come home."

"What do you mean?"

"They think maybe he was in the house."

"*In* the house! Oh, Willy!"

"Yep. I went back there soon's I brought 'em all home. Been there ever since; Herb Joyner and me milked. Ain't never milked before and it's quite a chore. Real tricky."

"Willy, you deserve some sort of medal. Have you had any sleep at all?"

"Nope, but I'll get it tonight. I ain't sleepy now. Anyways, like I said, Oren ain't showed up yet. I figure I ought to stick around over to Meeker's. Herb and me'll do what's necessary about the farm. Tell Mark that if he wakes up. Hope he don't wake up all day."

"I'll look after him, Willy," Mona said, her crossness forgotten.

It was two days before they found out for certain that Oren had been in the house all the time. The origin of the fire remained a mystery that was only guessed at. It was guessed at a great deal. Some people thought the fire had been set by one of Oren's enemies, for he had many. A few illogical ones insisted that the house had been struck by lightning, but nobody paid any attention to them. Until they found that he had carried no insurance, some others believed that Oren had set the fire himself and then been trapped.

There was no one to tell them the answer.

Who but the dogs had seen him, the night of the fire, coming unsteadily down the hill from the woods; fumbling at the catch of the rusty screen door, and once inside groping for the lamp and muttering? In all that dark storm-clouded valley, who was there to see the windows flower into light, and Oren sitting at the kitchen table, his drowsy head between his hands?

And hours later not even the dogs (since they were

shut outside) were there to see the lamp flame burning too high in its cracked glass flue, or to smell the scorching pages of the kitchen calendar hung above it, or to hear the wild, ever-strengthening crackle of fire set free.

Nobody saw, nobody heard. Not even Oren, who, head on the table, and jug upset beside his hand, was sleeping the deepest sleep of his life.

CHAPTER IX

Mark

It was Willy who told Mark.

Afterward he came into the kitchen where the Melendy children were sitting. They looked at him with scared, solemn faces.

"Now you stop lookin' like that," Willy commanded. "The end of the world ain't come. These things sometimes happen and you might's well know about 'em. It's Mark you gotta think about now. Oren was a rascal, and a villain, and a meanhearted sneak; but remember he was all the folks the poor kid had; I s'pose he got used to him the way a person gets used to chronic appendicitis, or boils, or any other hardship. He feels pretty lost right now, I guess."

"Where is he? Mark?" Rush asked.

"Leave him alone for a while. He's out back somewheres."

"Where will he go now? He hasn't anybody to live with," Mona said.

"Why can't he live with us?" cried Randy. "He could have the cupola, and he could teach us all to walk on our hands!"

"I'd take him fishing a lot," contributed Oliver, like an uncle. "It would help him take his mind off things." Mona couldn't help giving him a hug, which he instantly ducked out of.

"I know what I'm going to do," Rush decided. "I'm going to call Father long-distance, right now."

"To Washington, D. C.?" said Oliver incredulously.

"Well, I'm glad you thought of it," Willy said. "I was gointa suggest that myself; only wouldn't it be better to wait till tonight? You'd be more likely to catch him then."

"No, we'll do it now," decided Mona. "We'll take a chance."

They all went into the living room followed by Isaac and John Doe.

Rush lifted the receiver of the telephone.

"Hello, Miss Lederer. [Miss Lederer was the Carthage day operator.] This is Rush Melendy. I'd like to speak to my father in Washington, D. C."

They could all hear Miss Lederer's crisp, clicking little voice in the telephone. "Washington, D. C.! Do you know how much that costs?"

"Money is no object," replied Rush, like a prince of the blood.

"Does your papa know you're calling long-distance, Rush?"

"It's my father I'm trying to reach, Miss Lederer. Martin Melendy, Hotel Beauregard, Washington."

"We-e-ll." The little machine-voice sounded reluctant. "But the night rates are cheaper."

"This is urgent, Miss Lederer," Rush said.

By a miracle Father was at the hotel! Rush poured out his story from beginning to end. Father and Miss Lederer listened attentively.

"Keep him there, by all means! Keep him till I get up there next week. Then we'll see."

"Oh, you're swell, Father! I knew you'd say that—"

"I don't like to think of you being there alone. I'm so tied up here I can't possibly get away before next week. I'd better wire Cuffy to come home."

"Oh, *no*, Father! *Please* don't bother her. Willy's here, and we're pretty old now. Mona and I are anyway. We've got more sense than we used to have."

"We're getting old, too," said Oliver, and looked at Randy. "Aren't we?"

"Well, all right, Rush," Father said, at last. "I suppose you are growing up. I suppose you ought to be able to handle this situation. And you've got Willy, of course. Be good to the boy Mark; I know you will. Keep him company, don't let him worry. Tell him I'll look out for him when I come up. Now let me speak to Willy."

Willy took hold of the receiver as if it were a stick of dynamite. He had to clear his throat twice before he could speak.

"H'lo, Mr. Melendy," he croaked. "H'are you?"

The children listened to Willy tell the story of the fire all over again. They listened while he explained that he and Herb Joyner were looking after Oren's livestock for the present. They listened while he reported on their own behavior and state of health.

"Randy has a kind of little cold, Mr. Melendy. And Oliver don't go to bed early the way he oughta. He stalls, Mr. Melendy, something awful."

Oliver looked startled and guilty.

"Rush has been real good, and so have Mona and Randy. They're gettin' so they cook fine. Mark don't eat nothin', though, but I guess it's the shock. Lorna Doone's pretty good, though she got inta the corn last week and ate enough to bloat her. I mended the fence up back by the woods, and I'm buildin' a real good chicken house. Garden's okay: lotsa fresh vegetables and the corn's commencin'. Better come home soon, sir, we all miss you. All right, Mr. Melendy. You bet. Just a minute—"

Willy turned toward them and whispered (why no one knew), "He wants to say hello to each of you."

Mona was first. She gave him a list of all the things she had learned how to cook, told him about the play she was writing and the book she was reading, and the way the Scarlett O'Hara morning-glories were beginning to bloom.

Randy was next. She spent her time begging Father to come soon and telling him how they missed him. At the end she said, "Could you please bring me a pair of ballet shoes, size two? Pink satin?"

"Silly," said Rush, "there aren't any ballet dancers in Washington that I ever heard of. Just senators and congressmen, and they all wear congress gaiters, and very few of them wear size two."

Oliver shouted into the telephone, "HELLO, FATHER! THIS IS OLIVER. WHAT? YES. WHAT? OH. WELL, G'BYE."

Oliver hadn't talked on the telephone very often.

Rush finished the call, said good-bye again. Just as he said good-bye Miss Lederer chimed in, "Shall I send the bill to your home, Mr. Melendy? Or do you wish the charges reversed?"

Rush hung up. Father's voice without Father made him homesick for him. He looked at the others.

"Tough not having any folks at all," he said. "Come on, let's go find Mark."

They went outdoors. It was a beautiful day, sunny, with a wind blowing; but instead of bursting out with leaps and shouts, the Melendys came slowly, quietly. When they saw Mark standing beside the pool, with his back turned, instead of hailing him raucously and galloping across the grass, they approached deliberately, almost reluctantly. They were uncomfortable and full of pity and strange feelings. They didn't know what to say.

Mark said it for them. He turned around suddenly and smiled.

"I bet none of you can make a pebble skip five times across the pool."

Of course none of them could. In the first place, the pool was too small; in the second place, they couldn't make a stone skip five times even on an ocean. But they fell to trying eagerly; relieved, comfortable, noisy once more.

They had their own ways of showing him their good will. They made him take the first turn. They applauded passionately when he skipped a stone three times; and Oliver collected flat pebbles for his ammunition.

"What's your favorite thing to eat in the whole world?" Mona asked him suddenly.

"I dunno. Strawberry shortcake, I guess. I had some once when we were over to Carthage getting the reaper mended."

Mona's face fell. The time for strawberries was long over. Then she thought of something. "Did you ever taste *blackberry* shortcake? [Mona had never tasted it, either.] It's even better."

Randy said, "What's your favorite color, Mark?"

"Green is."

"Well, you know what? I'm going to knit you a green sweater. A good warm one."

"Gee, that would be wonderful. But I don't want you to bother."

"Yes," said Randy. "Green. With a neck and everything."

This was no mean contribution. Randy hated to knit and did it badly. She had never knitted anything except staggering, uncertain scarves, and the prospect of a whole sweater, with a front and a back and a neck, seemed as tortuous and difficult an undertaking as a journey through the labyrinth of the Minotaur.

"By Christmas it ought to be ready," Randy said, and couldn't help sighing. "Anyway, sometime before spring."

"Gee, that would be wonderful."

"Wait till you see it first," cautioned Rush. "It'll probably have three sleeves."

At lunchtime Oliver pressed upon Mark a seventeen-foot catfish line that Mr. Titus had given him: the pride of his heart. After lunch Mona went off in the direction of the blackberries with a basket in her hand, and Randy went to Carthage on her bike, allowance in her pocket, to buy green knitting yarn.

"Let's go for a hike," Rush said to Mark. "Someplace we've never been before. Someplace stiff like Powder Hill. Or let's take a long ride. Mona'd lend you her bike."

"I oughta go over t' the farm and see about things. He'd be awful mad if he knew I was loafing this way."

"Oh, come on. Willy's gone over to do your chores for you. Said he'd be glad to do 'em for the next few days. And Herb Joyner's going to milk."

"Well." Mark looked at Rush. "Gee, I never did ride a bicycle."

"I'll teach you then! Come on, we'll have a lesson now. You'll find out that it's like milking; not as easy as it looks!"

Riding a bicycle was not the only thing that Mark was interested in learning. He drank up new experiences like a thirsty weed. He was intoxicated by the Melendys' books, and sat hour after hour on the floor of the Office, surrounded with crooked columns of books that he had taken from the cases. Bowed over a volume, cheek in his hand, there was no sound from him except the frequent, dry turning of a page.

"This is a swell one. This is a good story," he'd say, lifting his head at last, and looking at the others with eyes still glazed by distance, still focused on the landscape of another world. "This boy, Tom Sawyer, he gets lost in a cave—"

Tom Sawyer, Robin Hood, Mowgli, Riki-Tiki-Tavi, Uncas, Long John Silver, all of them were new to Mark. Even the girls' books interested him: *Eight Cousins* and *Castle Blair* and *Sara Crewe*, even the old outgrown fairy tales with their colored pictures: *Water Babies*, *Hans Andersen*, *The Land of Oz*, the hundreds of satisfactory legends concerning the simple lad who wins the princess;

the thoroughly punished stepmother who dances in red-hot shoes, the witches, and godmothers, and emperors, and ogres.

Music fascinated him. Rush was astonished and gratified at such an audience. Mark would sit beside him on the piano bench by the hour; gazing at the hieroglyphics on the music book which were so skillfully translated by Rush's fingers.

"Play that one again," he'd say. "I like that one fine."

He liked them all; even the old chestnuts that caused the rest of the family to dash screaming from the room. And because they were new to Mark they became new to Rush too, and he loved them again as he had in the beginning.

But of all the new experiences the one which Mark learned most eagerly was the simple one of living in a family. At night when he went to bed in his windy tower he knew that there were other people near at hand, friendly and kind. He knew that when he woke in the morning there would be sun at the windows, a humming of voices in the house, a sound of water running, a smell of bacon cooking; and a day ahead that was full of jokes, discoveries, work, play, and conversation: full of new things to learn which he had never known or heard of. And he would leap out of bed as if there were not a moment to lose.

Under his ribs the hard, cold, fist-shaped thing that had hidden there for years became smaller, less and less, as if it were melting away, and in its place something grew and opened like the expanding leaves of a plant. Something warm and comfortable that tickled his ribs as it grew, and made him want to laugh a lot and be happy, and to see other people laugh.

CHAPTER X

Women's Territory

"Fold in sugar very gently, add one teaspoon of vanilla and a half teaspoon of almond extract," chanted Mona dreamily. "Pour into nine-inch mold, sprinkle lightly with chopped almonds, and—"

"Rub into the scalp thoroughly," concluded Rush unkindly. "Cat's sake, what *are* you talking about?"

"A recipe I got from Mr. Titus," Mona explained. "I memorized it instead of writing it down. That way I can't lose it. Bake in a slow oven—" she continued.

"Until the color and texture of grated charcoal," said Rush. "Garnish with nuts, bolts, and old washers, and serve one month later. What is all this, anyhow, Mona? First we have Shakespeare in big doses and now we have recipes. From *Hamlet* to omelet in practically no time at all."

"I have lots more," said Mona complacently. "How would you like to hear Mr. Titus's recipe for pound cake? I'll do it with dramatic expression this time. A pound of sugar!" Mona smote her brow and staggered a little. "A pound of butter!" She moaned as she said it. "A dozen eggs." Her voice dropped to a tragic whisper. "Four cups of sifted flour—" She opened her eyes with the mad smile of Lady Macbeth. "And two cups of RAISINS!"

"Okay, okay," cried Rush. "I'll eat it but I won't listen to it!"

For some time now Mona had been experimenting with cooking. It had begun, weeks ago, with a cake, which to her own surprise and everyone else's had turned out to be very good. It had gone on to a batch of popovers, to another cake (not quite so good), and thence to meringues. During each of these early experiments she had worked with furious concentration, cookbook propped before her, utensils and ingredients in mad profusion all about her, and a savage glitter in her eye. When the product in question had finally reached the sanctuary of the oven, Mona could be seen hovering before it anxiously, sniffing at the crack in the door, wringing her hands, all but praying.

"The murder suspect awaiting the verdict of the jury," Rush said.

She was remarkably lucky. The verdict was nearly always favorable, with now and then a healthy lapse such as that first rhubarb pie, a flat, flat raisin cake, and a sullen batch of doughnuts.

She pored over cookbooks, memorized recipes, lived in a daydream involving boiled frosting, melted shortening, egg whites. Her infatuation with baking led her to use up the last of the family sugar before the next ration ticket was due, and in consequence no Melendy had sugar on his cereal for a week, and every time Rush saw her he scowled darkly and muttered, "Let her eat cake!"

After that Cuffy had put her foot down, and Mona's fancy was confined to unsweetened foods such as soups, biscuits, and vegetables. She grumbled about this a good deal, but her interest continued. Now that Cuffy was away she allowed herself a free rein. Already there were three jars full of different kinds of cookies, and she was thinking of making a fruitcake.

"Listen, Mona," Rush said suddenly, a few days after the fire. "You'd better forget the delicacies for a while. Everything in the garden is getting ripe at once. Tomatoes turn red overnight. If they're not picked right away they just lie down on the ground and rot to get even. And the cucumbers! Jeepers, one minute they're the size of my little finger and the next they're junior-size blimps. What're we going to do?"

"We eat tomatoes for every meal except breakfast now," Randy said. "And the cucumbers are just getting boring."

"Maybe we could sell them," offered Oliver hopefully.

"Nix, small fry. In a rural community like this it would be coals to Newcastle."

"Canning is the answer," Mona said. "Oh, if only Cuffy were here!"

A moment later she looked up, striking the table with her mixing spoon.

"We'll do it ourselves! We'll surprise Cuffy."

"O-o-oh, no!" said Rush. "And have us all dead with bottling bacillus or whatever it is. No, thank you."

"Botulinus bacillus," corrected Mona. "Oh, Rush, don't be so stuffy. I'll get a book about it and do everything just the way it says. I'll only can safe things like the tomatoes, and I'll make pickles of the cucumbers."

"Gee whiz," said Rush. "Why did I bring it up?"

"And you'll help me, too. We'll begin tomorrow. You and Mark and Willy get the tomatoes and cucumbers; Oliver you wash them off outside at the hose fixture. Scrub them *good*!"

"Gee whiz," said Oliver, "I was going fishing."

"And, Randy, you can help me in the kitchen. Peeling and cutting things up and all."

"Gee whiz," said Randy. "I was going over to Daphne's."

"No, you'll all just have to help. I'm not any Little Red Hen," said Mona sternly. "Now I'm going to Carthage and buy some jars, and a book on canning and then I'm going to ask people about it: Mrs. Wheelright and Mr. Titus, and maybe the Addisons."

The last proved to be a poor idea. Mona came home with her head in a whirl of different canning methods.

"Gosh," she wailed. "They all swear by different systems, and I can't remember any of 'em. Mrs. Wheelright says open kettle, Mrs. Addison says oven, Mr. Titus says cold pack—"

"You better do it like Mr. Titus says," Oliver advised. "He knows all about food."

Mona slept an uneasy sleep that night, and her dreams were long dull dreams about tomatoes.

She rose early the next morning, got breakfast with Randy, and studied her canning book. By the time the boys and Willy began bringing the vegetables, she knew it almost by heart.

She and Randy were enthusiastic about the first bushel-basketful of tomatoes, it seemed a treasure trove: an abundance of sleek vermilion fruit, still beaded with dew. The second bushel also looked very pretty, the third a little less so, and by the time the fourth one arrived she stared at it with an emotion of horror.

"There *can't* be that many, Rush!"

"You asked for it, pal. There's the living evidence. And in twenty-four hours there'll be this much over again." He wiped his hands on his overalls. "And now make way for the cucumbers."

"The cucumbers!" Mona sank weakly into a kitchen chair. "I forgot all about them!"

There were two bushels of these. The kitchen was swamped with vegetables.

"I'll never laugh at any of those kitchen police jokes again," Randy said, about an hour later. She was standing in front of the washtub skinning tomatoes. "Look at these things! They skip right out of my fingers like live frogs."

"Here's the first sterilized jar," said Mona, in a hushed, scared voice. "Start putting 'em in, Ran. I'll get the juice to pour over."

It was a long, hot, clumsy business. Mona dropped sterilized lids on the floor, and they had to be sterilized all over again; Randy cut herself with the paring knife; Mona half-scalded her fingers getting the first jar into the boiler. Randy skidded and fell on a slippery tomato skin which had somehow landed on the kitchen floor. They lost two jars of tomatoes from the first batch when they were taking them out of the boiler. The first was dropped by Mona when she thoughtlessly took hold of it with her bare hands. The second exploded like a bomb, all by itself.

"I guess there was something the matter with it," said Randy brilliantly.

"We still have six left, anyway," said Mona. "And they look just like real canned tomatoes. I can't get over it!"

In the midst of all this, of course, Rush, Mark, Oliver,

and Willy came in, hungry for lunch. Observing the sea of glass and spilt tomatoes Rush assumed a murderous leer, and prowled to and fro growling, "BL-OOD! BL-OOD!" Then he stood up straight, frowned importantly, and turned to Willy Sloper. "Call Scotland Yard at once, Carstairs. Something extremely fishy has been going on here. A clear case of vegetable homicide!"

"Oh, Rush, it *can't* be noon," wailed Mona. "We've only *started.* We haven't even thought about lunch."

"They could have some cornflakes," said Randy helpfully. "And there are some cold noodles in the icebox."

"Cornflakes. Cold noodles," commented Rush. Then he crouched again. "BL-OOD! BL-OOD!"

"Cheer up, Mona," Willy said. "I got a frying pan and some eggs. We'll get some potatoes and have our lunch outdoors."

"Willy, you're swell," sighed Mona gratefully. "And maybe if there's anything left over—"

"Sure, we'll cook yours, too." Willy spoke over the loud protests of Rush, who was all for letting the girls languish on a diet of cornflakes and cold noodles. "Just like you suggested, Randy. Try mixing them with a little Rinso, and some catsup. M-m, boy, delicious! Try whipping them up with a couple of raw eggs and a dash of bicarbonate—"

"You get out of here, Rush! You're making me sick to my stomach," commanded Mona. "All of you go. This is women's territory."

"And the men can have it as far as I'm concerned," she added an hour or two later. "I never felt so hot and messy in my life. And all for a few old jars of tomatoes that will just get eaten up without anybody noticing."

Her face was scarlet with exertion. Her hair was tied up in a dish towel, and her apron was covered with tomato stains.

Randy looked worse if anything. There were tomato seeds in her hair and an orange smear across one cheek. She was wearing nothing but a faded old playsuit and an apron.

"Gee whiz," she said. "You know how I feel? I feel like an old, old woman about forty years old, with fallen arches."

"Still they look sort of nice. The tomatoes, I mean, not your arches. Look, Ran."

They were nice. Sixteen sealed jars of scarlet fruit, upside down on the kitchen table.

"Cuffy will be glad."

Mona nodded. They each sank into a chair; stared at their creations with the fond gloating of misers. Even as they stared and gloated another jar exploded. Hot tomatoes flew about the kitchen like larks, and so did bits of glass. Randy got a cut on the collarbone and Mona got a tomato in the eye.

At that very moment Mr. Titus appeared at the door.

To his everlasting credit, and the eternal gratitude of Mona and Randy, he didn't laugh at the spectacle confronting him. He didn't even smile. He just stood there, holding his shredded straw hat in his hand and said, "Thought maybe you might be able to use a helper. I knocked at the door and then I hollered. Guess you was too busy to hear."

"Mr. Titus, you're an answer to prayer." Mona was half in tears, and her eye hurt. "The flak around here is something fierce."

Randy gave Mr. Titus a hug. "Next to Father I'd rather see Cuffy, and next to Cuffy I'd rather see you come in here right now than anybody in the whole world."

Mona took his hat. Randy flew for one of Cuffy's big checked aprons; and in a little while the kitchen had turned from a cave of chaos to an orderly, efficient place. The tomatoes quieted down and allowed themselves to be canned submissively. They knew their master.

By six o'clock, in addition to three dozen perfect jars of tomatoes, there was a good supper cooking on the stove. Mr. Titus declined their invitation to stay and share it with them.

"No, thanks just the same. Got to get home. Got to feed Hambone. But I'll be by tomorrow. Around half past eight, maybe? Then we'll polish off the resta them tomatoes and get to work on the cukes. Dill pickles, maybe. I got some dill. And piccalilli and pin-money and mustard pickles. M-m, makes my mouth smart just to talk about it. I sure like pickles."

Rush watched Mr. Titus leave with awe. Then he turned and looked at his sisters for a moment.

"Women's territory, eh?" said he.

But even Rush knew better than to rub it in.

CHAPTER XI

"Welcome Cuffy"

The canning, like everything but beginner's luck, improved with practice. It also proceeded at fever pitch, since Cuffy was expected home on Saturday. The males of the Melendy household had a dreary five days of it, being hustled through breakfast, forgotten at lunch, and given any old thing for supper.

Daily at eight-thirty Mr. Titus arrived and presided over the culinary rites like an aproned Buddha. Randy and Mona, his handmaidens, peeled and washed vegetable after vegetable; hovered about the stove till their cheeks were crimson, opened the oven door and frowned in at the contents, lifted the lid of the enormous boiler on top of the stove releasing great steaming fogs; and gradually on every hand appeared the result of their labors. Jars upon jars of tomatoes, of tomato juice, and yellow tomato preserves. Jars of dill pickles and of India relish. While the fever was on them the girls spent their pocket money (and whatever they could wheedle out of Rush and Oliver) on crates of peaches and plums, and put up quarts of each. Intoxicated by the great sacks of extra canning sugar which Cuffy had stocked, they went even farther; experimenting with jams and conserves.

Each morning they got up early, eager to be at work. Each night they staggered upstairs glassy-eyed with fatigue, the kitchen clock ticking loudly under Mona's arm. Upon its dial its shocked hands might be pointing at anything from nine o'clock to quarter to eleven. Promises to Cuffy concerning early retiring were temporarily suspended.

"After all, it's what they call an essential industry," Mona justified it to Randy.

"Well, maybe the vegetables and the fruit. But plum and apple conserve? And blackberry jam? Do you think they'd be called essential?" Randy was tired. She was going upstairs on all fours like a dog.

"Yes, I do," replied Mona firmly, and that was that.

On Friday night they finished. Mr. Titus went home

with six assorted quarts in a basket and the lifelong gratitude and devotion of Mona and Randy credited to his account.

That night, the alarm clock stayed in the kitchen and kept its mouth shut in the early morning. Mona and Randy slept the well-deserved sleep of hard workers, and in spite of the gagged alarm clock woke from force of habit at six-fifteen and stayed awake. When Mona, shoes in hand, crept down the stairs to the kitchen she found Randy there before her, sitting on the high stool in her blue pajamas and yawning, while an egg bubbled and hissed in the frying pan.

"I wonder if we're going to keep on waking up at dawn like this for the rest of our lives," said Mona.

"I like it. The day feels so unused."

Sunshine lay against the wall in pinkish bands, and out of doors a late-nesting wren sang its bubbling clear song.

Mona got an egg for herself. Pausing on her way back to the stove she looked out the window. The dew was so heavy on the grass that all the lawn was coated lightly with silver. There was blue in the shadows and Willy's sunflowers were hanging their heavy yellow heads; if they had had faces they would have looked like the flame-fringed suns in old Russian fairy tales.

"Summer's almost over," sighed Mona.

"Oh, don't say it. Don't say it! I don't want it ever to end."

"Neither do I. But it will; and in the middle of September I'll be working on the radio again."

Mona couldn't help smiling as she pried her egg loose from the pan. It would be fun to go back to work. To be acting again, to know again the exciting blend of make-believe and reality. To study anew the art of her profession; to work, and learn, and try to make a perfect thing of the part she played. Yes, and to be flattered a little once more. Mona's vanity rose and arched itself like a small cat, purring in anticipation.

Randy was eating her breakfast looking gloomily at nothing. She hated to part with each passing moment; and now, in the realization that it was nearly over, the summer gained a poignant value. How had it slipped away, carelessly expended, gloriously wasted? She had planned to try to make perfume out of honeysuckle and rose petals; and now it was too late. The honeysuckle was over long ago. She had been going to learn all the different bird songs. But now almost every bird had stopped singing. When had they stopped?

"Well, I'm not going to waste any more of it!"

"H-m-m?" said Mona, still smiling. She was thinking about her fan mail.

"Ow!" she exclaimed indignantly a second later. "The bacon spat at me. Ouch. I've got a burn on my wrist. Where's the soda, Ran?" Once more chance circumstance had given a tweak to her vanity.

"What aren't you going to waste any more of?" she asked, patting soda and water on her offended wrist.

"The summer," Randy explained. "I'm going to appreciate it. I'm going to walk in the woods noticing everything, and ride my bike on all the roads I never explored. I'm going to fill a pillow with ladies' tobacco so I can smell it in January and remember about August. I'm going to dry a big bunch of pennyroyal so I can break pieces off all winter and think of summer. I'm going to look at everything, and smell everything, and listen to everything so I'll never never forget—"

"You know what Cuffy tells you, Randy, whenever you begin hating to have things change, something about the way 'blessings brighten as they take their flight!'"

"But why shouldn't they?" argued Randy. "If they didn't brighten just when you're about to lose them you'd never appreciate them. You'd just live from one day to another, not knowing or caring about anything, like—like a turnip."

"Turnips care deeply about many things," remarked Rush, appearing suddenly. "Turnips are strongly emotional vegetables; and anyway what's Randy doing recommending change when she always says she hates it?"

Randy, baffled, retired from the field.

"I don't know, Rush, I'm all mixed up. You're too smart for me."

"Maybe I ought to get a job with the Quiz Kids," said

Rush thoughtfully, and he began assembling his favorite breakfast; the one he always ate when Cuffy wasn't there to stop him. First he ate a large bowlful of Grape-Nuts with brown sugar, cream, and a sliced peach. Then he made a sandwich out of two thick slices of toast, butter, marmalade, and bacon. Then he made another, adding peanut butter for variety.

"Where's Mark? Where's Oliver?"

"Mark was in the shower when I came down," Rush said. "He spends hours in the shower; he can't get over it. I suppose it's because he never saw one before. Oliver's still asleep, the little slug. Mr. Titus coming again today?"

"No, we're all through canning."

"Halleluiah!" said Rush. "Now we can take up the broken threads of our lives once more, and eat a good, hot dinner in the middle of the day."

"But look at the job we've done, will you?" cried Randy. "Just *look* at it, Rush. We've left it all out for Cuffy to see!"

Rush nodded slowly. "It's something!" he agreed.

It was something. The quart jars were arranged on the shelves, and the windowsills, where the light could best reveal their amber, purple, and vermilion splendor. In front of the quarts stood the pints; filled with pickles and preserves.

"How beautiful they are," sighed Randy. "I hate to think of eating them."

"Not me," Rush said. "I can hardly wait for winter."

"I wonder where Mark will be this winter," remarked Mona. "I wish Father would come home and decide things."

"I wish he would, too. And I wish Mark could just go on staying with us forever," said Randy wholeheartedly.

"He's a swell guy, all right," agreed Rush. "He knows more about the names and habits of plants and animals and things than anybody I ever saw. Did you know that grouse like to bury themselves in the snow in wintertime, for instance? Did you know that a bee dies after he stings you? And that there's a star called Aldebaran? And that around the tenth of August, any year, you can look up at the sky at night and see dozens and dozens of shooting stars? Have you ever seen a plant eat an insect? I have, right in Bagget's pasture, in the boggy place. Have you ever seen a dragonfly grub? Or a geode? Did you even know there *was* such a thing as a geode? I didn't, either. I learned about all those things from Mark."

"Maybe *he* ought to join the Quiz Kids," Mona said wickedly. "I'd like him even if he couldn't tell all about bugs and things. I just like him because he's nice, and doesn't think he's smart the way some people do. He's good, without being too good, you know, and kind of sensible but fun, too."

"Sh-sh, here he comes," warned Rush. "He'd hate to hear all the slush we've been talking about him."

Mark came in, scrubbed and shining. Mona broke another egg into the pan.

"Gee, I'm late," Mark said. "Half past seven! I never ate breakfast so late in my life!"

"I hope you're not getting soft," Rush said.

"It's the farm I'm thinking about. Farmers can't afford to sleep late."

"Or to fool around in luxurious shower baths half the day," added Rush, and Mark reached across the table and almost succeeded in pushing his face into the marmalade.

For the last four days Mark had been spending a large part of his time at Oren's farm trying to keep up with the work. Willy helped him when he could, and so did Rush and Herb Joyner. When it came time to cut and stack the field corn and do other heavy jobs there would, of course, be still more volunteers; but even so the work was hard and demanding and continuous. Mark said little about it, but the Melendys sensed his underlying feeling of anxiety and responsibility.

"I certainly do *wish* Father would come home," Mona repeated, almost angrily. "I bet the President of the United States, and Congress, and everyone, could figure things out by themselves for a couple of days. Just for a couple of days! If they'd just let him come home for a mere, simple weekend!"

"Mo-na!" called a rumpled voice from somewhere upstairs. "I can't find my snee-kers!"

"Oh, dear," cried Mona, as she ran out of the kitchen. "They're probably outdoors, soaked with dew, or they've fallen into the brook or something."

After breakfast Rush and Mark departed for Oren's farm. Oliver went to the garden and Mona and Randy set about cleaning house so that it would look nice for Cuffy.

"It's terrible what a state the place got into while we were canning," groaned Mona. She had her hair tied up in a towel, and was wearing one of Cuffy's aprons wrapped around twice, and she looked awful. "How do you suppose people do it? Real housewives with children and all?"

Randy shook her head, at a loss. "When I grow up I'm going to be a famous painter and dancer, and live in a hotel."

"And I'm going to be a famous actress with lots of flowers in my dressing room. I'll live in a hotel too."

"We won't ever have to cook anything."

"Or can anything."

"It was fun, though."

"Yes, thanks to Mr. Titus. Won't Cuffy be pleased?"

"And surprised?"

"Absolutely thunderstruck. Oh, dear," said Mona, "I wish I weren't so scared of the vacuum cleaner. I hate the way it swells up and roars the second I press the button."

"I know. And the way it sort of insists on going where it wants to. I'll take turns with you, though."

The house hadn't been swept or dusted for a week. Mona and Randy rushed about feverishly, dusting the same surfaces twice, sweeping little heaps of lint into corners and forgetting about them, misplacing cleaning cloths, and repeatedly allowing brooms and mops to fall with sharp clatters to the floor. The vacuum cleaner buzzed all morning like a mighty bee, and Randy and Mona called to each other above it, like people in a multitude.

At noon Mark, Oliver, Rush, and Willy trooped into the kitchen with expectant faces. Smiles dying as they looked, they saw only a lifeless stove, devoid of pots and pans, and a bare table with no signs of the preparation of food. The floor was clean and empty except for Mona's two shoes, one a little in front of the other, exactly as she had stepped out of them hours ago.

"This is too much," said Rush. "This is too much!" He leaped like a maddened Mohawk through the door toward the sounds of buzzing and shouting which were issuing from upstairs.

"—WITH CURLS ON TOP," Randy was braying loudly.

"I LIKE IT LONG," Mona brayed back. "SORT OF TURNED UNDER AT THE ENDS. PAGE BOY, THEY CALL IT."

"Page boy," repeated Rush in disgust as Mona turned off the vacuum cleaner. "Page boy! Why not bellboy, or busboy, for heaven's sake? And *where's our dinner?*"

"Oh, my," said Mona, letting the vacuum cleaner fall beside the prone broom and mop. Rush really did look pretty mad. "Is it noon already?"

"Noon! It's half past twelve, and you have four dangerously hungry men on your hands. We could forgive scarce meals while you were canning, but now there is no excuse!"

"Scrambled eggs," hissed Randy, "they're easy, and I'll make a salad."

"Eggs," groaned Rush. "You're always falling back on eggs. I've eaten so many since Cuffy's been away that I'm beginning to grow pin feathers."

After a hastily assembled meal they all went back to work. Gradually the house regained its normal expression: a look of reasonable order, and unprosperous but homely comfort. Rush had brought in flowers and Mona arranged them; great armfuls of zinnias, petunias, marigolds, and coreopsis. Willy was even prevailed upon to cut some of the lesser sunflowers.

"What am I ever going to put them in?" pondered Mona. "They're so huge."

In the end the only container large enough to hold them proved to be a small aluminum garbage can. Mona hid it tactfully behind a leather tuffet, and above it, against the living-room wall, the sunflowers blazed in a fiery constellation.

Cuffy's room was a regular bower. Oliver contributed to it an arrangement of his own: wild flowers stuffed into a kitchen tumbler, vervain and clover and black-eyed Susans, all picked too short and rather wilted from the firm grasp with which he had held them.

"Those flowers say Oliver all over. I'll put them on the table by her bed," Mona said, and removed her own tasteful bouquet of late moss roses and forget-me-nots in a little white vase.

Through the open windows came a sound of lawn mowers. Rush had borrowed Mr. Titus's and Willy was using the Melendy one, and they were performing a sort of double concerto on the grass. Every time they met, pushing and rolling, Rush would say, "Ships that pass in the night," or "Dr. Livingston, I presume," or "There's a lawn, lawn trail a-winding," or some other silly remark. Isaac gamboled about Rush and barked frantically at the mower, which kept spraying grass at him. John Doe gamboled and barked about Willy's mower. It was noisy, rather pleasant work.

Oliver was cultivating the vegetable garden. He hoed and raked, hoed and raked, and now and then pulled up a fat purslane plant, first killing it with an imaginary machine pistol. "D-d-d-d-d-d-d-d-d-d- Pow-oo. Pow-oo. Got him!"

Drops of perspiration flew out from under Oliver's hat, but the song of the crickets cheered him on, and the tall, stout sunflowers stood about him like a gathering of friends.

Randy had washed all the week's canning-stained dish towels, and they flapped mildly on the clothesline, adding an odor of Clorox to the summer air. She had also scrubbed out both the bathtubs, and was now frantically trying to bring order out of the chaos that was Rush's room. It was a masterly confusion of bird's nests, snakeskins, books left open facedown, sheets of music, symphony scores, war posters, disbanded chemical sets, microscope lenses, fishing tackle, old letters and postal cards, and odd stamps which had escaped from his stamp album. A hammer and saw, some nails, a bottle of varnish, and an empty Coca-Cola bottle with a straw in it were among the articles on the bureau, and on the bed were two old comic books, a model airplane, and a volume of the life of Beethoven. As Cuffy had predicted, shoes and articles of clothing were draped about the floor. Rush no more had the instinct to hang up his discarded clothes than a snake has the instinct to hang up its shed skin. It nearly drove Cuffy mad.

Among the shoes and clothes were scattered pages of lined music composition paper. At the top of each was written "Opus III: Sonata in E Flat"; underneath in smaller letters were the words "by Rush Melendy," and at the left, still smaller, the words "Largo Maestoso."

"Goody," said Randy, seeing this. Largo Maestoso was her favorite tempo. It was the tempo of funeral marches, which she enjoyed, and also it was easier to play than things like scherzo and allegro. You had time, between chords, to think what you were going to do next.

All the music sheets contained notes. Some only a few, some a great many, but none of the pages was completed. The notes scampered frantically up and down their lines like black pollywogs, and across one of the sheets there was an angry scribble, and the words "This stinks" written in red pencil.

Randy did what she could with the room, which, since time was getting short, consisted largely of stuffing things into drawers and closets. When she got fed up she leaned out the window and yelled at Rush.

"I don't care if you're a genius or not, you'll just have to clean the rest of your room yourself!"

Then she went up to the Office and painted a big poster saying WELCOME CUFFY. Around these words she painted angels with harps. All the angels looked like movie stars, it was only by the wings that you could tell.

Heavenly smells came from the kitchen. A kettle of leek and potato soup was simmering on the stove, and in the oven a cake was performing its fragrant mystery. Mona had mopped the floor, the quart jars of preserves glowed like somber jewels on the windowsill, and the alarm clock ticked with that sure, contented sound that one hears only in well-ordered kitchens.

The Melendys were pleased with their day's work. They had a right to be.

"Now all we have to do is to get clean ourselves," Mona said. "I'm going to wear my new white dress."

At five o'clock Willy hitched Lorna Doone to the surrey, stuck two red zinnias into her bridle, and drove her around to the front door.

"Come on, all," called Willy. "Time t' go meet Cuffy."

Randy climbed down from the railing. She had been pinning the welcome sign up over the front door. She had on a clean yellow dress and was wearing shoes and socks for a change. The other children appeared, one by one, all unusually well-groomed.

"I wish Mark could have come with us," Randy said.

"Well, he has to milk," Mona told her. "And anyway I think he felt kind of—you know—delicate about it."

They piled into the surrey. Isaac and John Doe wanted to go, too, but they were not allowed. They sat side by side on the doormat under the welcome sign and stared reproachfully at the departing surrey. Isaac's lip was tucked in sulkily: he thought for a moment or two of running away again and giving everybody a good scare, but then he remembered the skunk episode, and abandoned the idea. He lay down flat with a thump, gave a sigh like the air going out of a blacksmith's bellows, and glared at the world. He would have nothing to do with John Doe, who sat upright beside him tongue hanging rakishly out of the side of his mouth; his eyes, nose, and ears joyfully alert to possibilities.

Lorna Doone clip-clopped along the highway, her mane blowing in the summer wind; the whip glittered in its holster, the fringes tossed. No one talked. They had all worked hard and were comfortably tired. Autumn was coming soon, all right. The air was full of thistledown and milkweed floss, high in the sky, low, skimming the grass, all flying, all traveling: shimmering in the sunny air like phoenix feathers.

The mullein had finished blooming, and stood up out of the pastures like dusty candelabra. The flowers of Queen Ann's lace had curled up into birds' nests, and the bee balm was covered with little crown-shaped pods. In another month—no, two maybe—would come the season of the skeletons, when all that was left of the weeds was their brittle architecture. But the time was not yet. The air was warm and bright, the grass was green, and the leaves, and the lazy monarch butterflies were everywhere.

"I wonder if she's changed," mused Oliver.

"Who?" said Rush.

"Cuffy. I wonder if she's changed."

"In two weeks? I doubt it."

"Heavens, is it only two weeks?" cried Mona. "It feels like months or years. Think of everything that's happened. The fire, and—Oren, and having Mark with us, and learning to can, and all. I feel years older."

"I wonder if Cuffy'll think *we've* changed," said Rush, rather taking to the idea.

"I doubt it," Willy said. "Look 'bout the same to me, all of you. Course Oliver's lost a tooth. And maybe you're a mite thinner, Rush—"

"It's the meals I've been getting," Rush sighed. "No, but I mean in our characters."

"Oh, characters," Willy said. "Well, time'll tell, time'll tell. When you're a kid your character's kinda quick an' easy, bendin' this way, that way, changin' itself overnight. 'Tain't set yet. When you're old it's set, all right, and there ain't nothin' to be done. You got it like you got the shape of your bones. Maybe you've lost all your hair, and then again maybe you mighta lost your nerve. Maybe you're farsighted when you look at the paper, and kinda nearsighted when you look at the truth—"

"Maybe you have flat feet, or a flat sense of humor," interrupted Rush. "Maybe hardening of the arteries, or hardening of the heart. And then you could have either a false set of teeth or a false set of values, or both. Gee, I could keep this up for hours. Willy, you should have been a preacher. That was quite a sermon."

"Aw, quit," Willy said. "Remember you ain't got no character at all yet. It's still just growin', bendin' this way an' that way. Nothin' but a little jellyfish still."

"Jellyfish! Listen, I've got a strong character! Why, listen, I—"

"Nothin' but a jellyfish," repeated Willy peacefully. "All of you. Just a lot of little jellyfish."

"Some jellyfish sting, don't forget," said Rush.

He stared at Lorna Doone's tail and wondered about his character. He was sure he had a strong character but when he began to think hard about it there didn't seem to be anything to take hold of. Am I generous? wondered Rush. I guess so. But only when I want to be, so I guess I'm not. Have I a good disposition? Yes, except when I'm mad and then it's fierce. Gee, remember the time I threw the tapioca at Mona and she had to have her hair washed; remember the time I socked fat, old Floyd Laramy; remember the time I—but no, better not think about disposition. Am I talented? Rush brightened a little. Sure, he was talented. He played the piano better than any kid he'd ever heard, he earned money giving lessons, didn't he? And he composed music, what's more. He began to think about Opus III: Sonata in E Flat. He kept getting stuck in the middle of it. Stuck and still stucker; he couldn't seem to pull out of the bog. He thought of the sheet on which he had scribbled, "This stinks." Oh, nuts to character.

"Oh, nuts to character!" Rush said out loud.

"Well, at least you're a good athlete," said Mona. "And you understand a lot about music."

"Yes, and you know how to make people laugh. I wish I did," said Randy, and Rush realized that he was not the only one who had been analyzing his own character.

In fact Oliver was the only person who hadn't been. He was sitting contentedly squashed between Rush and Willy, smelling Lorna Doone's lovely smell and dreamily imagining himself in the act of catching a twelve-pound catfish, just like Mr. Titus.

CHAPTER XII

The Principle of the Thing

The Braxton station looked just like any other medium-sized station. It was a long, low, ugly building, flanked by a long, low, ugly platform. The black and white sign saying Braxton stuck up from the edge of the roof like a ticket in a hatband.

There were a few people on the platform already, staring vacantly at the two pairs of railroad tracks which stretched endlessly away to the right and to the left, straight and shining as the strings on a giant banjo.

Mona and Willy stayed in the carriage, Oliver climbed up on an empty baggage truck which at once became a landing barge. Randy and Rush went inside the station.

It was a stale, brown place, with a slot machine, a magazine stand, and a cast-iron stove that looked as if it had been there since the Civil War. A long bench, worn smooth with the sitting of multitudes, ran round the wall, and behind the ticket window a narrow-faced man in a green eyeshade seemed to be doing sums in a book.

"All stations smell exactly alike, I wonder why," Randy said. "I could be led in blindfold in a large city, and I'd know it was a station right away."

"Yes, and there's always a man behind the ticket window that looks just like that," whispered Rush. "I don't think they're really alive. The railroad companies probably order them from Sears, Roebuck, or someplace: 'One ticket agent, complete with sleeve garters, and eyeshade—$24.98.'"

Randy went over and looked at the magazine stand. All the comic books had names like *Biff*, *Crash*, *Bang*, and *Boom*. All the photography magazines had names like *Pix*, *Flix*, and *Nix*. The candy bars in their paper wrappers also had interesting names such as "Nummy Bar" and "Vita-munch." Randy looked at them longingly, but she had no money.

Rush had a penny. He dropped it into the slot machine, pulled a lever, and waited for something to come out. Nothing came. He pulled the lever again. Then he started to bang the side of the machine and shake it.

At this the man in the eyeshade came to life, or at least his voice did.

"That never does any good," said he, without looking up. "Everybody always tries it and it never does any good."

They stared at him.

"Why, has it been out of order a long time?"

"Yep. Quite a while, now, quite a while. Since March, April, I guess."

"Well, it's a gyp," grumbled Rush. "It's not the loss of a penny that I mind. It's the principle of the thing."

Randy liked the sound of that.

"I bet lots of people have lost pennies in that machine," she said. "And it's not right. They probably don't mind about the money so much. It's the *principle* of the thing."

"Well, I been after the fella to fix it. After him and after him, but he keeps puttin' it off."

"I should think you could fix it yourself," Rush told him, "with a pair of pliers and a screw driver."

"Daresay I could. But like you said, it's the principle of the thing." The ticket agent looked up from under the eyeshade and smiled at them. He had a nice smile.

"Listen," suggested Randy. "Why don't you just paste a little sign on the machine saying 'out of order' or something?"

"Never thought of it," confessed the ticket agent. "But it ain't a bad idea. I'll take care of it right after I'm finished with the five-forty-five. Thanks for the suggestion, and as soon as she's fixed I'll see that your money's refunded."

"Oh, that's okay," Rush said.

And Randy said as they went out, "I bet Sears, Roebuck would never sell him for only $24.98. He's too nice."

There was a sudden change among the waiting people on the platform. One minute they were drooped about their suitcases, yawning, shifting from foot to foot, longing to say good-bye; and the next they were alert, straightening quickly, and smiling. "It's coming! It's coming!" Suitcases were picked up, hats straightened, kisses bestowed upon cheeks. All of them, the ones who were leaving and the ones who were staying, looked far, far along the humming tracks toward the tiny black feather of smoke. All felt the same small stab of excitement. Something is going to change, something will be different in a minute.

Oliver tumbled down from his landing barge, Willy and Mona leaped from the surrey. Mona took Oliver's hand, and suddenly felt Randy take hold of her other one. They stood close together watching the engine approach, growing larger and larger; towering above them with its Cyclops eye and its mane of smoke. Together they winced in the terrible moment when it flew past them, hot as a hundred furnaces, and loud as a burst volcano. Its fiery breath blew their hair, rocked them on their feet, and filled their eyes with cinders. It was heaven.

The passengers began descending.

"Where's Cuffy?" Oliver kept bleating, over and over again. "Where's Cuffy? I don't *see* her, Mona, where is she?"

"Oh, goodness, Oliver, sh-sh. She'll be coming out in a minute, give her time."

"Well, but where *is* she?"

All they saw of her at first was bundles. A whole solid façade of nothing but bundles. Then they saw the familiar bulging "satchel" hanging from her arm.

"Cuffy! Cuffy!" shrieked Oliver, beside himself, leaping and jumping. And then as he glimpsed her face, "She hasn't changed! She hasn't changed!"

But who was that behind her?

"Father!" yelped Oliver, by this time in a frenzy of joy.

They all were. They threw themselves upon Father and Cuffy. Father submitted helplessly, his arms weighted down with suitcases, and bundles were knocked off Cuffy.

"Great day!" she cried. "There goes the fruitcake!"

"Fruitcake!" Rush pounced. "How *is* Cousin Coral, by the way?"

"Recovered," said Cuffy. "And talked out for the next year, I should think."

"How were the poodles?"

"Dreadful. Fat and spoiled. Made me real homesick for Isaac and John Doe."

Willy and Rush took charge of the suitcases, and such bundles as they could handle.

"Father!" said Mona. "There's a long pink ribbon hanging out of your briefcase. What in the world is it?"

Father looked down at Randy. Randy stared at the pink ribbon, and then at Father. Tremendous joy took hold of her.

"Ballet shoes!" she said, almost in a whisper. "Oh, Father!"

It was rather congested in the surrey. Cuffy sat in front with Oliver on her lap. Father sat in the back with Mona on one side and Rush on the other, and Randy on *his* lap. Suitcases and bundles took up the rest of the room.

"Do you have to go away again on Sunday night? Can't you just this once stay over, for a little while?" Randy asked the question more as a matter of routine than as an expression of hope.

But Father said, "Yes, as a matter of fact. This time I can stay over."

"You *can*?" cried everyone. "How long can you?"

"Three weeks."

Three weeks. Three whole weeks! Boy. Jeepers. Gosh. Hooray. Halleluiah. How divine.

"What will the President do without you?" Oliver wanted to know.

"Oh, he has my telephone number," Father said grandly.

The town of Braxton dissolved unnoticed into the green fields and woods. The surrey seemed to fly. Everyone talked. Father had to be told all over again about Mark, the fire, the farm, and all the rest of it. And he in turn had to tell them about Washington and the people he saw. Cuffy had a lot to say concerning Mrs. Theobald and the poodles and Mrs. Theobald's friends. Willy reported upon the progress of the hens, the goat, Lorna Doone, and matters in general.

They were home before they knew it.

"Why, look," cried Cuffy. "A welcome sign! Now, isn't that just lovely!"

"Only if I'd known you were coming I would have put 'Father' on it, too," said Randy. "You know I would have, don't you?"

"Sure, I know it," said Father, and gave her a squeeze. "I'll be glad to get you off my lap, just the same, both my knees are asleep. How many pounds have you gained, anyway?"

As they were disentangling themselves and their luggage from the surrey, the front door opened and Mark came out. He had on a clean shirt that Rush had given him, and clean overalls, and his hair was still rakemarked from the comb. He was wearing his only shoes, too; big, bump-toed work shoes from which he had scraped the mud, and even made a stab at polishing. Seeing how he had made a great effort to present himself at his best, Randy felt an ache of sympathy. Let Father like him. Please let Father like him, she prayed inside. Cuffy was safe, no use wasting a prayer on her. She liked Mark already.

Mark came forward smiling his shy, friendly smile.

"Why, Mr. Melendy came too!"

"Yes, isn't it swell! Father this is Mark Herron."

Father took Mark's hand, and looked into his face.

"How do you do, Mark. I've heard a great deal about you."

Mark looked steadily back at Father and smiled again. "Gee, Mr. Melendy, I sure have heard a lot about *you* too!"

"We'll have a talk by and by," Father said, and went into the house. Randy, skipping along behind with the fruitcake held tight against her chest, felt her heart lighten. Of course it's too soon to tell, she thought to herself, it's much too soon to tell, but I *think* it's going to be all right. I think he likes him.

And Rush coming up beside her suddenly whispered, "I think he likes him, don't you?"

That was the wonderful thing about Rush. He so often seemed to feel the way she did. How many girls had such a satisfactory brother?

Aloud she only said, "Yup," and then she made a leap and a pirouette, and tossed the fruitcake right up in the air, because she couldn't help it.

"The house looks real clean," said Cuffy in a tone of surprise. "I wouldn't of dreamed it would look this clean."

"It *is* clean," Mona said. "Run your finger along the banisters, Cuffy. Examine the baseboards. Look under the piano. The whole house is impeakable."

"Impeccable," corrected Rush.

"Okay, impeccable. And now—come out in the kitchen, Cuffy," said Mona quietly, almost trembling with excitement. "Father, you come too."

They all came, even Willy.

Cuffy pushed open the swing door and looked about her. The long rays of sun had lighted up the jars of preserves on the sill till they glowed like the glass in a church window.

"My lands," said Cuffy. She went over to the sill and then to the shelves, picking up a jar here and there, and reading aloud from the labels. "Chowchow. Yellow tomato preserve. India Relish. Peaches. Plums. Plums. Plums."

Then she came quietly over to the table and sat down on one of the wooden chairs. They watched her, disappointed.

"What's the matter, aren't you glad?" said Randy.

"Glad. Glad!" Cuffy gulped pathetically. "Why, when I think of you poor little things, all by yourselves, doing all this wonderful canning. Why, I could just lay my head right down on the table, and—"

"Don't you do it, Cuffy, don't you do it!" cried Oliver, who had a horror of tears. He leaped onto her lap and tried to tickle her.

"All by yourselves, all that hot work!" murmured Cuffy brokenly.

"Well, Mr. Titus helped," said Mona uncomfortably.

"*Helped!*" Rush gave a hoot. "Mr. Titus took over. The girls *helped*. You better save your tears for the rest of us, Cuffy. We haven't had a decent meal in days."

Oliver gave up trying to tickle Cuffy. She was wearing her "good" corset which was as unyielding as the armor plating on a tank.

Anyway Cuffy felt better after she'd heard about Mr. Titus. She blew her nose and went back to examining the jars.

"Fine color," she'd say. "Couldn't have done 'em better myself. Dill pickles: hm-m, wonder where he got the dill? Glad you put up all them tomatas. I'll put up a few more quarts myself, and we oughta have enough to last . . ."

They left her musing over the canning, and went out to conduct Father on the usual ceremonial grand tour. They showed him the sunflowers, and the big green footballs in the watermelon patch, and the red-stained apples that were bending the branches of the orchard.

As they were coming back across the grass Father said to them, "I'm very pleased with the way you've all done your jobs. The place looks fine: the lawns are smooth, the garden well-kept, the house clean, and then all that splendid canning! Yes, I'm very pleased. The way you've taken hold these past weeks shows real character."

Rush walked close up to Willy and spoke to him quietly. "Jellyfish, huh?" was all he said.

"And though the quality of all your work is excellent,"

Father was continuing, "and I am delighted to see that it is, I would still be happy even though the job had been amateurishly performed. Because it's not only the quality of the work that counts at a time like this. It's—"

"The principle of the thing!" shouted Rush and Randy in a bold duet.

CHAPTER XIII

The Best Birthday of All

Father did like Mark.

"Of course I really always knew he would," Randy said. "Way down deep I knew it. I was just sort of ruffled on the surface."

"You couldn't help liking Mark," Rush said. "He's good. I don't mean good *acting*. I mean good material all the way through, like a—a good potato or something."

"Potato, for heaven's sake!" cried Mona. "He's much more interesting than a potato. He's—let's see, Randy, what sort of vegetable *would* you compare him to?"

And the discussion turned into one of the Melendys'

favorite games, known as the comparison game. It went like this: somebody left the room, or at any rate went out of earshot. While he was gone the rest of them decided upon a person known to them all, either by fame or by personal acquaintance. When the one who was "it" came back he was allowed only to know whether this mysterious subject was male or female. Then he asked his first question: "What color is he like?" After he had been told he asked the next person: "What animal is he like?" Or what vegetable, bird, jewel, flower, or tree. Even what kind of weather. It was surprising how interesting it was, and how quickly one could guess the identity of the person in question. Cuffy's color, for instance, was unmistakably white; and she was like a pigeon, and like a pussycat, and like a pearl, and like a big, healthy cabbage rose. Oren, on the other hand, had been compared to a weasel, a chicken hawk, a parsnip, and the color of mustard yellow.

Mark turned out to be good Golden Bantam corn, a setter dog, a meadow lark, a maple tree, and many other pleasant, reasonable things. They had left Mark by now, though, and were describing what seemed to be the most fascinating creature in the world. She was a female, and Randy and Rush (Oliver scorned this game) agreed that she was like a velvety, purple pansy, like a dark sapphire, like a song by Brahms (Rush contributed that, of course) . . . Mona was "it" and she wondered secretly, and hopefully, if the person in question might not be herself.

They had played it that way once or twice just as a joke on the unsuspecting questioner.

"What sort of vegetable is she like?" asked Mona, with a self-conscious toss of her silky hair.

It was Randy's turn to answer.

"Oh, not like any vegetable in the world! Never, never like a vegetable!"

Mona's hopes flagged. Once long ago they had used Mona for the subject, and they had agreed, quite easily, that she was like a cucumber. A cucumber! It was the sort of thing you could never forget.

But Rush did not see eye to eye with Randy. "She is like an onion," he said dreamily. "This person is like a very smooth, white, pearly onion."

"*Rush*!" cried Randy. "An *onion*! How can you ever, ever say such a terrible thing!"

The battle was on, and of course the character turned out not to be Mona at all. It was Hedy Lamarr.

At this point Father's voice was heard calling them.

"Where are you all, anyway?"

"In the Office, Father, do you want us?"

"No, I'll come up. What are you doing?"

"Oh, just fighting," Mona said. "But it's not serious."

Father came up the stairs. He looked around the Office.

"Where's Mark?"

"He went over to Oren's farm."

"Good. I hoped I'd catch you alone." Father declined to

sit down. He stood up, with one elbow on the piano, as though he were about to make a speech.

"Have we done something bad?" said Oliver.

"No, no. Or at least not as far as I know. It's about—"

"Is it something about my birthday?" inquired Oliver. "Would you like me to leave the room?"

"No, not this time. You can stay. As a matter of fact, it's about Mark."

"Oh."

They waited. Father picked up a sheet of music and looked at it carefully without seeing it. He put it down again.

"What do you think of Mark?"

"Why, we think he's swell. We think he's just about the swellest guy we ever met," Rush said. Mona and Randy agreed ardently, and Oliver said, "Did you know he can walk on his hands?"

"I see. And what do you think should be done about him?"

"Why, Father!" said Mona. "That's what we were going to ask you!"

"*I* know what should be done about him," announced Oliver. "He should just go on living with us."

"Oliver's right," Randy said. "That's what we all think. Couldn't we sort of adopt him?"

"Or really adopt him?" added Rush.

"If it's going to be too expensive, we can do without allowances," Randy said.

"You can have practically *all* my radio money for his support," offered Mona wealthily. "I'll only keep enough for train money and ankle socks and things."

"And I'll get more piano pupils when school opens, and I can contribute, too," said Rush.

"Mark will be a help, too," said Oliver, who was a very practical boy. "He knows a lot about farming."

"And he can teach us all about nature," added Randy enthusiastically. "He knows *everything* about it. We'll learn all the right names of funguses—"

"Fungi," corrected Father absently.

"—Fungi, and insects, and plants. He'll teach us all about trees and birds and—uh—*nature*."

"Won't that be nice?" pleaded Oliver in such a desperate voice that Father couldn't help laughing. Nobody else laughed, though. They sat there, silent and beseeching, their imploring eyes upon his face.

"*Please*, Father!" entreated Randy.

"He'll have to go to an orphanage, or be adopted by strangers, or something, if you don't," threatened Rush.

"Well," said Father, at last. "It's a serious step to take, you know. It's one thing to adopt a baby, and another thing to adopt a thirteen-year-old boy."

"It's better," said Mona positively. "It's better because he can talk and walk and all, and he doesn't have to be fed by hand."

"And you have a good idea of how he's going to turn out, too," agreed Rush. "With a baby you'd never know.

Why, it might grow up to be dishonest, or stingy, or mean to animals!"

"I'm not worried about the way Mark is going to turn out," Father admitted. "It's all there in his face: honesty, and courage, and dependability. He knows how to work too, and he's intelligent."

"There, you see?" cried Rush. "He'd even be a good influence for us!"

"Well . . ." Father sat down on the piano stool, and reflectively touched a key: E flat. He held his finger on it, and the sound died away slowly, quivering on the air as it diminished. When they could no longer hear it, Father took his finger off the key, and turned around and faced them.

"But perhaps he won't want to be adopted."

"Father!" shrieked Randy ecstatically, and flung herself upon him. Rush said Father was swell, Mona said he was divine, and Oliver demonstrated his approval by jumping up and down rather heavily and saying. "Oh, boy! Oh, boy! Oh, boy!"

Father shook them all off, finally, and stood up. "I think I'll take a walk over to the farm and have a talk with Mark."

"Are you going to tell him now?" asked Randy. "Are you going to invite him to be adopted?"

"Formally," replied Father.

"What about Cuffy? Maybe she won't like it," said Mona.

"Cuffy will like it, all right," Father said. "She's been hinting at it for all she was worth for the last two weeks."

"Oh, Father, you're a wonderful man!" sighed Randy.

"At times I'm inclined to share your opinion," agreed Father, going down the stairs.

The Melendy children were so happy that they became quiet. Mona picked up her radio script and tried to study it. Oliver opened a book. Rush sat down at the piano and began playing softly. Randy climbed the steps to the cupola. It was very neat up there. The bed was smoothly made, the few clothes were hung up, and the bump-toed shoes stood exactly side by side in front of a chair, like the feet of an uneasy visitor. Mark will be a neat brother to have, thought Randy. She looked out the north window toward Carthage. In winter it will be too cold up here, she thought. Then he can have Clarinda's room. It will like to have somebody living in it after all this time.

Suddenly Mona had a dreadful idea. She came right out with it, interrupting Rush's music, Randy's reverie, and Oliver's third laborious reading of *Dr. Doolittle*.

"Maybe he *won't* want to be adopted!" she said. "Maybe he'll be too proud or independent or something. Maybe he'll say no!"

"Don't be a goon!" Rush told her crossly. "Of course he won't say no."

All the same the mood was spoiled. He started to play again, but this time he galloped into the Brahms

Rhapsody, which was splendid music for restlessness or doubt.

It seemed hours before Father and Mark returned. They waited anxiously. Randy had gone up to the cupola again, and was the first to see them. There they were, coming down the drive. Father's arm was around Mark's shoulders and Mark was looking up at him, smiling and talking, nineteen to the dozen.

"What do you see up there, Sister Anne?" called Rush.

"It's okay!" shouted Randy joyfully. "I see them coming, now, and they look related as anything!"

But it turned out that the business of taking Mark into their family was not quite so simple as it seemed at first. The Melendys, it appeared, could not just pick Mark up like a stray puppy and bring him home with no questions asked. Questions were asked about everything, and by many different people.

First of all, there was the bank. The Carthage Bank had a most tender interest in the mortgage attached to Oren's farm. The State Department of Social Welfare had an interest in the destiny of Mark Herron. So had the county Children's Aid Society. Also there were sundry inquiries from private persons, such as the Delacey brothers, Cedric and Fitzroy, who wished to know the plans for the Meeker dogs and a certain Hampshire shoat among the livestock. Others inquired about the cows. Herb Joyner, Mr. Addison, and several other farmers wanted to engage Mark as hired boy. And there was even one elegantly worded document from a certain Waldemar Crown, offering all the comforts of his home to "this luckless child, this lonely orphan, deprived by ruthless circumstance of each child's birthright: the security of a home, and the guidance of a mature mind."

"Oh, yeah?" said Rush, when Father read him the letter.

"It sounds like a cross between a sermon and a campaign speech," Father said. "Who *is* this gentleman?"

"He's just an ordinary, everyday murderer and bank robber. At least that's what they say," Rush explained airily.

"Oh, that's all, is it? Just one of the many drones one meets in the daily grind. And speaking of meeting, what's your connection with the fellow?"

"Maybe I'd better tell you." Rush sat down and told Father the story of the still from beginning to end. Father looked almost cross.

"Listen, you young idiot, do you know you might have been peppered full of buckshot? Maybe seriously hurt? Don't ever let me hear of such an escapade again, understand?"

"Don't worry, Father," said Rush. "There's not a chance. I'd never stick my neck out like that again."

The first person to come and call on them was a Mrs. Golding, a children's worker from the Department of Social Welfare. Father received her in his study, and during the course of their conversation was interrupted four times. Once by Oliver, appearing with a large sheepshead which he had caught right in their own brook.

"I had quite a time getting him in," said Oliver sociably, holding up the fish and allowing it to drip on the carpet. "You see, the line got caught around a dead branch that was sticking out of the water there, so I just thought I'd better wade right in and untangle it. Well, I did that, and *then*—"

"Yes," said Father. "That's fine, Oliver, but perhaps you could tell me about it later."

"Oh, I have plenty of time right now," said Oliver cheerfully. "And maybe this lady would like to hear about it."

"*Later*, Oliver," Father told him firmly, and Oliver finally took the hint and started for the door. Just before he reached it, however, he turned and addressed himself to Mrs. Golding. "It's especially lucky that I caught this good big fish today. Because today is my birthday, and I'm eight years old." He waited for Mrs. Golding's congratulations, received them graciously, and departed with his fish.

Father and Mrs. Golding continued their interview for some time, then suddenly past the partly open door drifted the unself-conscious figure of Mona. She had a strange dreamy expression on her face, was wearing a wreath of nasturtiums and carrying nasturtiums in her hands. She looked straight ahead of her like a sleepwalker, and as she walked she lifted one of the flowers and remarked in an eerie voice: "There's rosemary, that's for remembrance:

pray you, love, remember: and there is pansies, that's for thoughts. There's fennel for you, and columbines: There's rue for you: and here's some for me: we may call it herb of grace o' Sundays . . ." She floated out of earshot.

Mrs. Golding was obviously startled. Indeed, she seemed alarmed. Father looked at her uncomfortably.

"My daughter Mona," he explained. "She's really quite sound mentally, in spite of appearances. It's simply that she has every intention of becoming the American Sarah Bernhardt, and lately we've had to put up with great doses of Ophelia. That's the Mad Scene you just saw," he added, perhaps unnecessarily.

Mrs. Golding was an understanding soul. She laughed till the tears came.

The next interruption was caused by Randy, who came in to ask for twenty cents.

"I need another ball of yarn for Mark's sweater," said she. "And I'm already overdrawn on my allowance."

Father hastily fished a quarter out of his pocket and gave it to her. Randy held up the half-finished green sweater and showed it to him.

"I have such a terrible time with dropped stitches," she said, turning confidingly to Mrs. Golding. "Every night I find new ones and have to rip out yards of it. I feel like the wife of Ulysses ripping up the shirt every night, except that I haven't any suitors. Yet," she added thoughtfully.

"Run along now, Randy," said Father, who was beginning to be embarrassed by the friendly volubility of his children.

As Randy left he turned again to Mrs. Golding. "Now as I was saying, in regard to the boy's education—"

At this moment Isaac and John Doe burst into the study, ran rapidly around it twice with their tongues hanging out, and departed, leaving the rugs all up in lumps.

Father sighed, "Well, as I was *saying*—"

But Mrs. Golding closed her notebook and dropped it into her briefcase.

"Never mind," she said. "I know already everything I need to know about Mark's future home. But I would just like to have a look at the boy himself."

"Of course," said Father. "There he goes now." He pointed to the window. Mark was wobbling along the drive on a pair of stilts. Rush was close beside him on another pair. They had made them yesterday afternoon, when it was raining.

"Pretty soon I'm going to tie the tops of these things tight to my waist, and see if I can walk without holding onto them," Mark told Rush.

"That's the way circus clowns do," agreed Rush, suddenly collapsing on the gravel.

"I'll call Mark," said Father, standing up. But Mrs. Golding said, "No, after all, don't bother. He looks as if he were having a thoroughly good time, and," she added, smiling, "something tells me he's going to go on having it. He's an extremely lucky boy."

"We're an extremely lucky family," Father told her. "Mark is a fine person."

They went out the front door where Oliver was cleaning his fish on a copy of the Carthage *Post-Clarion*.

"If you're considering a legal adoption, of course, you'll have to take it up with the surrogate's court," said Mrs. Golding.

"We'll let Mark decide that."

"Sorrow gate's Court, Sorrow gate's Court," sang Oliver mournfully to himself, fish scales flying about him. "I'll never go back to the Sorrow gate's Court. Never, oh never, oh never, oh never, back to the Sorrow gate's Court!"

When Mrs. Golding's capable-looking little blue coupé had disappeared around the bend of the drive, Randy stuck her head out the upstairs window.

"What did she say, Father? Is he really ours now?"

Father looked up and smiled. "If he wants to be."

"Gee whiz!" cried Randy, and an instant later she galloped down the stairs, shot out the door past Father and across the lawn to where the boys were stiltwalking. Her impulsive hug flung Mark from his stilts, but fortunately he was not seriously hurt. Mona and Oliver followed Randy at almost the same pace, and Rush leaped from his stilts and began clapping Mark on the back so hard that he made him cough.

"We all belong to the same family now! The same family!" shrieked Randy, dancing around them.

Mark escaped from them finally, and crossed the lawn to where Father was standing.

"Are you *sure* that you want me, Mr. Melendy?"

"We're sure, Mark. Are you?"

"Me?" said Mark. "Oh, boy!"

He looked, Rush said afterward, as if he had swallowed a lighthouse.

As all this coincided with Oliver's birthday, Mona made a suggestion.

"Let's have a double celebration! And let's have it a picnic party instead of just a plain dining-room party," she said. "We'll take Oliver's presents with us, and the cake too. We can eat the ice cream when we get home."

There was some discussion as to where they should go until Rush remembered the cave of which Mark had once spoken.

"Could we go there? With all the baskets and stuff?"

"Sure, we can ride part of the way, and then it's just a short walk through the woods."

It was a warm, golden September day. Cuffy and Mona and Father and Willy went in the carriage with all the dishes and presents and food, and the birthday cake carefully shut up in a hatbox of Cuffy's that had the name La Petite Yvette written on the side of it in dashing green handwriting. Everybody else went on bicycles, even Mark, for Mona had lent him hers. He was rather a wobbly rider still, but getting better. Isaac and John Doe licketed along beside the bicycles, and Lorna Doone stepped gaily.

Mark led them along an unfamiliar byroad, and after they had traversed it for a mile or two, he halted them and said they must walk the rest of the way. They tied Lorna Doone to a tree with plenty of grass around it, ambushed the bicycles, and each with his load struck off into the woods.

"Thought you said it wasn't a long walk," grumbled Rush, under a burden of baskets, blankets, and thermos jug.

"Never *seemed* long before," Mark said, sweating under a similar burden. "Course I never took it with a load before."

Cuffy brought up the rear, carrying the birthday cake in its hatbox. She walked slowly, turning her head away from twigs and leaves with a look of loathing. Cuffy liked nature to be confined: mowed, tied back, and kept neat, as in a backyard. She had no use for the unmannerly tendrils, undergrowth, insects, and general inconveniences of untamed woods.

The last straw was a short, steep, struggling climb up a sharp, densely wooded hill. They slid, clutched, panted, and groaned as they went up it. The paper cups were jolted out of Mona's basket and rolled all the way down again, to her disgust. Willy grasping at vines desperately said, "Sure hope none of these is poison ivy!" And Cuffy, her neat grey hair caught up in selflocks, gasped, "Sure hope it's worth it when we get there!"

They reached the top of the hill, descended a little way

and found themselves standing upon a broad sandstone ledge.

"This is it," Mark said.

And after all it was worth it. On this side the hill fell away abruptly, down and down into a ravine. There were birch tops at their very feet, and the vermilion berry clusters of mountain ash. As far as the eye could see were folded, wooded valleys, one opening into the next, endlessly and harmoniously. Above in the blue sky were mighty cumulus clouds; great weightless continents hanging motionless in the air.

"Jeepers!" said Randy, and Rush gave a long, low whistle. Cuffy sat down hard on a rock, fanned herself with a paper plate, and remarked that she was real fond of views.

"But where's the cave?" demanded Oliver, turning to Mark.

"Look," Mark told him, "turn around."

Oliver turned. Close against the cliff grew a dense blue hedge of juniper.

"I don't see anything except just big bushes."

"It's sort of prickly," Mark said. "But follow me."

He pushed right in among the junipers, and Oliver followed, saying "Ouch!"

"Mark? Where are you, Mark?" he called suddenly, but Mark had disappeared. He pushed on a little farther, the prickly branches snapped together behind him, and he found himself standing in a natural doorway in the rock. It was dark in there, a dark secret place.

"Mark?" said Oliver doubtfully.

"Come on in," whispered Mark, out of the shadows.

Oliver stepped in. It was instantly much cooler and stiller, and there was a very dark, damp, thousand-year-old smell. The junipers made a blue screen that cut out much of the daylight.

"Let's startle 'em a little," whispered Mark. "Yell your own name good and loud and see what happens."

Oliver opened his mouth wide and yelled his name. Instantly echoes woke up all over the cave. "Oliver Oli-ver-ver-ver!"

"Now yell 'help!'"

Oliver bawled obediently.

"Help-elp-elp-elp-elp!"

There was a crashing and an ouching outside. Rush's face stared in at them without seeing.

"You in here?"

"Come on in and yell," invited Oliver. "It's much better than the tunnel in Central Park."

Mona and Randy appeared after that, and the cave rang with war whoops and strange greetings.

"Hello-o-o. You-oo-oo. Goon-oon-oon!"

Isaac and John Doe contributed to the eerie pandemonium by a great deal of amplified barking. Father and Willy finally pushed their way through the junipers to see what was going on, but Cuffy stayed where she was. She had no use for caves. "Nasty damp places," she said. "Why don't they just go down and holler in the cellar? Can't see the difference."

Father and Willy had brought their flashlights. The turning circles of light revealed the rough rock walls and the sandy floor of the cave, which was littered with nutshells, cherry pits, bits of dry bone, and feathers. There were paw prints here and there, and some long sweeping marks that Mark said had been made by snakes. Isaac and John Doe stepped about eagerly, noses to the ground and tails quivering with excitement. A great deal had gone on in this cave.

Father said, "How did you ever find the place, Mark? It's so concealed."

"One time I got caught up here in a storm, Mr. Melendy. It was a real bad storm, the sky just split wide open and let go with everything it had. Hail, too. And it was big hail, and it hurt just like stones would hurt. So I squeezed in under the juniper bushes, but gee it was so scratchy I kept on pushing back and back, hoping maybe there'd be a kind of a little pocket between the bushes and the rocks. First thing I knew I'd pushed myself right into the cave. Boy, was I ever surprised!"

"Sure is a lot of bats hangin' up there," observed Willy, whose flashlight was trained upon the ceiling. They all looked up. What had at a first glance appeared to be a thick growth of moss or fungus now proved to be a community of bats. Here and there among them were little motions: the shifting of a claw, the stretching of a wing, the turning of a small, eared head. And now that everyone was silent, little sounds could be heard as well: the faintest rustle, and a tiny nickering.

"How revolting!" shrieked Mona suddenly, and plunged for the door. Randy, shrieking too, close at her heels.

"Girls!" remarked Rush, with patient boredom. "They probably look just as bad to the bats. Say, Mark, have you ever found anything here? Like Indian relics, or human bones, or counterfeit money, or anything like that? Or maybe old weapons, or a secret map, or something? In books people always discover stuff like that in caves."

"Yes, that's what I always thought, too. But all I ever found was an old cowbell."

"Maybe you didn't look hard enough," Rush persisted. "A place like this is too good a hideout for *somebody* not to use. Maybe we ought to dig up some of the sand. No harm in trying. Why, if I were a robber I'd be sure to bury stolen goods in a cave like this."

"Well, you kids search, if you want to," said Father. "You can have my flashlight, but not too long, I don't want the battery worn out."

He and Willy pushed through the juniper screen again. Oliver went with them. He did not care much for bats himself.

Mark and Rush searched the cave diligently. Then they went to work with sticks, scraping away at the sandy floor.

"I tell you what!" cried Rush. "We ought to use this for a hideout ourselves. We could keep things here, you know. We could keep cans of food, and crackers in a tin box, and bottles of ginger ale, and stuff. Sometimes you and I could camp out and stay here all night!"

"Not a bad idea," agreed Mark excitedly. "We'll make it into a real camp. We can gather lots of dead wood and stack it in here. Then we'll always have firewood. And we can bring some books and comics, in case we feel like reading."

"Yes, and some candles, and a knife to protect ourselves with—"

The time flew, and great plans were laid. Sticks scraped fruitlessly in the sand, and overhead the bats stirred and twittered restlessly in the unaccustomed yellow light.

"Come and *get* it!" shouted Randy, in the midst of it.

Out of doors a fire had been lighted on the ledge; the plates and cups were all set out, and Randy and Mona and Father were roasting hot dogs over the flames.

The party was a great success. The birthday candles dipped in the air, and Oliver liked all his presents. He was particularly fond of the creel Father had given him; the large supply of peanut-butter fudge contributed by Mr. Titus, and the set of willow whistles, all different sizes, made by Mark. And the Melendys' old friend, Mrs. Oliphant, had sent him a big, gorgeously illustrated book on moths.

Oliver, as usual on such occasions, grew pale and could not eat, but happiness was nourishment enough.

They stayed until the sun went down. And then a spooky thing happened. The bats began coming out of the cave. By dozens, in a steady stream, they dodged out between the juniper twigs, fluttered and swooped above the fire, circled and zigzagged in the twilight, with tiny, sharp squeaks. There seemed to be hundreds of them, and they flew close, close about the people on the ledge. They could feel the air fanned against their faces.

Mona threw herself flat on the ground and covered her head with her arms. Randy flung herself against Father and buried her face in his coat. Oliver flung himself against Cuffy, and Cuffy grabbed the first thing she saw, which happened to be a picnic basket, and put it on her head, with the handle under her chin.

"They never really do get into people's hair, Cuffy," Father said. "It's just a superstition."

But Cuffy refused to remove the basket. She sat there proudly with it on her head, one arm around Oliver, like some strange African tribeswoman or priestess. Only after every bat had disappeared would she take it off.

They had quite a time going down the hill in the dark. The lurching light of the flashlights made everything appear larger than before; and there was a great deal of slipping and stumbling. The tin cups and forks clattered in the picnic baskets, and Oliver got the hiccups. Everyone was relieved when they at last reached the road where Lorna Doone and the bicycles were waiting patiently.

But there was still more to Oliver's birthday. When they came home, they ate the ice cream. Then he said good night. Shortly afterward he came flying down the stairs in his underwear.

"Going someplace?" inquired Rush.

"My Cecropia!" panted Oliver. "It's my Cecropia! It's hatched, come and see! Come and see!"

"His what?" said Cuffy, as they went up the stairs.

"His moth," Rush said. "The one that used to be that big green job with all the buttons when it was a caterpillar. He must be a freak. He's six months too early."

They came into Oliver's room, all of them, and there, on the curtain, was the beautiful thing. It had wide, velvety wings with red borders, and broad, fringed antennae. In the middle of each wing was a mark like a Persian crescent.

Oliver stood gazing at it, gratified as though he had created it with his own hands.

"It's wonderful!" he sighed. "It's almost as wonderful as my luna."

"What luna?" said Rush.

"Oh, just a luna I saw. Father, isn't he *beautiful*?"

"Perfectly beautiful, Oliver."

"Cuffy, isn't he *beautiful*?"

"Real pretty," Cuffy had to admit. "My lands, it's a good thing he isn't the kind that eats clothes, though, being the size he is."

"Are you going to let him go?" asked Mona.

"Yes, right now. I want him to have a good time before the nights get too cold."

Oliver caught him in a little net, and started out of the room.

"Oliver!" cried Cuffy. "*Not* in your underwear!"

But Oliver kept right on going, the other children behind him. They went out onto the dusky lawn, Oliver opened the net; the great, soft creature crawled out onto his finger, hesitated a moment, and then fluttered away, vanished in the darkness.

Mark, watching, thought: I was like that. All folded up tight in a cocoon, dark and uncomfortable, and now I'm out of it, like him, now I'm free. Naturally, he didn't voice this sentiment. It would have sounded corny. It would have sounded so corny, in fact, that he got hot thinking about it, gave a great war whoop to get his mind off the subject, and chased Rush into the house.

When Oliver and Mona had gone in too, Randy took a short walk.

She had the world to herself. It was very dark. Everything frightened her a little; the moving shadows, the melancholy sighing of the spruce trees. A falling leaf touched her cheek softly, and she jumped. She came upon the sunflowers sooner than she expected, and they rustled faintly, like tall people breathing. They frightened her, too. She turned and walked back toward the brook.

The earth seemed to quiver, and sing, and vibrate with

endless insect sounds. The scent of ladies' tobacco drifted down from the pastureland near Carthage. At the far end of the lawn Randy turned and looked at the Four-Story Mistake. The windows were all open, and most of them were lighted. The house was like a big, airy lantern. A sound of talking came from it, and a sound of running bath water. Up in the Office Rush was practicing his Schumann, and out in his rooms above the stable Willy was tootling on his recorder. Randy listened to all these familiar noises, and in addition she heard the hollow voice of Mona's radio, a single, querulous bark from Isaac, and the woodpecker tapping of Father's typewriter. The house hummed with life.

She could see things happening in it, too. There was Cuffy walking to and fro past Oliver's window. Putting away his clothes probably, and picking out clean ones for tomorrow. Up in the Office Rush was playing the piano, and Mark was sitting near-by, listening, and scratching his back with a pencil. Down in the study window Randy saw Father's beloved head, in profile, studiously bent above his typewriter, the reading glasses far down on his nose.

Randy played a game with herself that she had sometimes played before. She played that she was a stranger, a wanderer in a foreign land, who had come upon this house unexpectedly, after a long and lonely journey through a forest.

She stood in the shadows and looked at the way the light from the windows lay in long rectangles on the grass; she listened to the many noises, and watched Cuffy moving about in her comfortable way, the two boys at the piano, and Father at his desk.

Randy sighed, a lonely pilgrim's sigh. The people in that house are happy people, she thought, and felt a stab of longing. That was the thing about this game. It seemed so real, and the sense of relief was so marvelous a moment later when she told herself, That's *your* house, dopey. That's *your* family, and you're part of it!

She ran quickly across the grass and jerked the front door open so hard that all the little moths were jarred off the screen.

She ran upstairs to Oliver's room. He was sitting up in bed in blue-striped pajamas, surveying his birthday presents for the last time till tomorrow.

That is Oliver Melendy, my brother, thought Randy, staring at him with her stranger's eyes. He looks like a nice boy.

"Did you enjoy your birthday, Oliver?" she asked him.

"Yes, I did," he replied. "It was the best birthday of my whole life, and I got almost everything I wanted, except a helicopter, and I didn't *really* think I'd get that. And I caught that good big sheepshead, and my Cecropia hatched out, and I got a new brother that isn't a baby. Yes," Oliver said slowly, as though carefully weighing the value of each of his birthday events, "I guess that was really the best thing that happened to me today: getting Mark for a new brother."

CHAPTER XIV

Admit One

Oren's farm went to the bank for mortgages. The little that was left over had to be spent on his old debts. Mark saw the farm go without regret. With its burned buildings, black skeleton tree, and eroded gully full of debris, it seemed to stand for all the castoff wretchedness of his past life. Let it go, thought Mark, let it all go. I never want to see it again as long as I live.

"The livestock, though," Father said. "It all belongs to you now. You were Oren's only relative as far as we can find out. You now have seven cows, a team of work horses, a pretty good Hampshire boar and sow, and sixteen pigs and some chickens. Also some dilapidated farm machinery. What shall we do with it all?"

"Could I make you a present of a cow or two, Mr. Melendy?" offered Mark, as if he were proffering chocolates. "How about the pigs too? I'd like it fine if you'd take 'em *all*!"

"Nobody ever offered me a cow before," replied Father thoughtfully. "I'd like a few, very much. There's not enough heavy work on the place for a team, though, and I don't honestly think we need pigs. Perhaps Willy would be grateful for some more hens."

So after that there were three cows at the Four-Story Mistake. They lived in the stable with Lorna Doone, Persephone the goat, and her daughter Persimmon. In the morning, after milking, Rush or Mark drove them out to pasture. In the evening Oliver fetched them home again. From lean cows with peaked joints and barrel-stave ribs they became round, queenly cattle with a dignified and measured gait. Their bells tinkled all day long, and from time to time a distant sound of mooing could be heard, as if someone were blowing into a conch shell.

As for the remaining Meeker livestock, it was Mona who thought of what to do about them. "Auction them," she suggested. "But let's auction them here. We'll have—*I* know!—We'll have a kind of fair. We can have a show, maybe, and sell something or other; for the benefit of the Red Cross, or something. (Except Mark's cow money, he'll need that for himself, of course.)"

Everyone thought this was a splendid idea, combining all the best features of business, pleasure, and good deeds. The date was set for the middle of September, a Saturday. Father promised to come home for it.

For his three weeks' vacation was at an end. His bags were packed, his briefcase dusted off and bulging with its own importance once more. Also he was returning to his labors with an added six pounds of weight and a healthy tan.

"If only you could always be here," sighed Mona, her cheek against Father's scratchy sleeve. "We'd all have such a good time, and you'd never get that green, crumpled look again."

"Green, crumpled look, eh?" said Father. "Must be what they call Pentagon Pallor. Ah, well, one must sacrifice something even if it's only beauty."

"Father, you're so *silly*," Mona said, and gave him a hug.

It was sad to have him go. It was always sad. But this time they had many things to occupy their minds. There were plans for the Fair. And then there was school.

School began the day after Father left. The children looked different that morning. The girls wore clean sweaters and skirts. Everybody wore shoes and socks, their hair was brushed smooth for once, and all were clean. Isaac and John Doe prowled around the breakfast table distrustfully. "Where are they going now?" the dogs asked each other. "What is the matter with them? All their shoes smell of polish!"

After breakfast there was a tremendous lot of hurrying and dashing up and downstairs, and collecting pencil boxes and copybooks. At last they were ready. Willy drove the surrey around to the front and they all piled in.

Cuffy stood on the doorstep, issuing last-minute commands and admonitions. "Oliver, *use* your handkerchief when you need it. Mona, you see he drinks all his milk at lunch and see that Mark does too. Randy, stop leaning out like that. Rush, *Rush*, you didn't take your sweater—"

But the surrey was halfway up the drive. "Too late now, Cuff!" called Rush, free as air.

"Lands, lands, them *young* ones!" muttered Cuffy, going into the house. How big it was, how empty. The air seemed still to ring from all the recent haste and noise.

Isaac sat down in a patch of sunshine and scratched at his ear with a loud, boney thumping. Then he went to sleep. Cuffy stood in the middle of the living room, lost in thought. Suddenly she turned, hurried to the broom closet in the hall, and dragged out the vacuum cleaner with a clatter. She couldn't stand the silence.

But by the next morning she was used to it, and even rather liked it.

As for the children, their lives were frantically busy. At school there were new teachers, new classrooms, new faces, new books. And after school there was homework, and there were long, thrilling conferences about the Fair.

It was to be a Children's Fair, Mona decided.

Everything about it was to be done by children. She, and Daphne Addison, and all the girls they knew would bake cakes, cookies and candy, to sell. The boys would take care of putting up the decorations, building the booths, and so on. There were going to be grab bags too, and a fortune-teller, and a show. The Melendys adored giving shows.

In the afternoons when they came home they took their homework as if it were castor oil, gulping it down as fast as possible, and immediately afterward plunging into the important matter of the Fair.

Mona (who was to be the fortune-teller) wandered about with a Cheiro palmistry book, practicing on the palms of her family. She was always grabbing somebody's hand and saying, "You're going to live to be a hundred. You'll always be safe in accidents. You're going to have five children. Or do those lines mean that you're going to be *married* five times?" And then she would look in the book to make sure.

"You have a good, even head line," she told Willy Sloper. "And your heart line's nice and steady, but *this* thing—well, I don't know exactly what it is, but I know it means something extremely interesting. Just wait till I look it up in the book—"

"It means I peeled a potato the wrong way thirty years ago," Willy said bluntly. "It's a scar."

Randy practiced dance steps for the show. She also painted posters. Already there was one in the Carthage post office, one in the school gymnasium, and another over at Eldred, in the bank.

AUCTION AND FAIR! *[the posters said]*
3 P.M. SEPTEMBER 18
FOUR-STORY MISTAKE.
LIVESTOCK TO AUCTION.
CAKE SALE AND CONCERT.
ENTERTAINMENT AND REFRESHMENTS.
COME ONE, COME ALL.
Tickets 50 cents. Benefit of Red Cross.

Oliver made the tickets. He cut them out of cardboard and printed the words "Admit One" on each, in colored crayon. He made so many of them that at night when he closed his eyes he kept seeing everywhere the words "Admit One."

Rush and Mark did a lot of striding about with hammers and nails, though actually there was little to be built. Mona was going to use the summer house for her fortune-telling; the animals were to be tied up in the stable (except for the pigs, of course), and the Addisons had contributed two tents for outdoor booths. Still there were some boards in the stable, and Rush and Mark both liked to build, so they made a pavilion down near the brook; rather lopsided, it was, but large, and a splendid place for a cake sale.

"Decorations, though," sighed Mona. "There's nothing

but crêpe paper, and not much of that. I even looked when I was in the city. And of course balloons are out of the question, and I suppose Japanese lanterns are unpatriotic, even if we could get them. So what *shall* we do?"

Their solution was given them, however. None of them ever knew who had whispered their problem into the benevolent ear of their old New York friend, Mrs. Oliphant, but one day, about a week before the Fair, a large box arrived for them.

"It's awful light," said Oliver dubiously, lifting it. "Awful light for anything so big, and it doesn't rattle."

"I wonder what it can be," wondered Randy.

"The best way to find out is to open it," said Rush, and swooped down on the cord with his scout knife.

There was a rapacious pulling and tearing, and a growl of torn cardboard.

"Look, here's a note," announced Rush, holding it up over his head where nobody could reach it. "No, let me read it out loud. Saves time. 'Dear Children,' it says. 'I hear you are in need of decorations and am sending you these. I bought them in San Francisco's Chinatown, years ago, because I knew, intuitively, that the time would come when I would surely need them to beautify a Livestock Auction. I wish I could be present on the momentous day, even though I could not promise to buy a cow or even a pig, since the apartment is crowded already. Much love to you all, including the new member of the family. Gabrielle DeF. Oliphant.'"

"Hooray for Mrs. Oliphant!" shouted Oliver. "Next to Cuffy she's the nicest lady I ever saw."

"And look at the decorations!" cried Mona.

Almost speechless, they carefully took them from the box. There were great, pleated garlands, and necklaces, and chains, all made of paper. They opened out like fabulous accordions, many feet long, and were most marvelous colors: green, turquoise, yellow, vermilion, magenta, purple. There were dozens and dozens of them, all different shapes and colors, and beautiful beyond the wildest fancy. There were gilded paper dragons, too, and fantastic, scowling fish, and curious masks. These were ornaments fit to fly from the minarets of Aladdin's palace.

"Oh, brother," said Rush. "This is going to be the prettiest Livestock Auction and Fair that anybody ever saw!"

"It mustn't rain!" said Mona. She looked up at the sky severely. "It must not rain!"

As the day drew near, a sort of quivering excitement seemed to vibrate over the Four-Story Mistake, exactly as intense heat makes the air quiver above a prairie. Dozens of strange bicycles lay dead on their sides in front of the house each afternoon. Children were everywhere. There was a sound of hammering, of laughter, argument, and loud conversation. A smell of baking floated out of doors. Vast preparations were under way in the kitchen, though the cakes themselves had to be made at the very last.

There were difficulties, of course. Rush smashed his thumbnail with the hammer and worried for fear it would affect his playing. They could not agree as to the best place to give the show. Pearl Cotton, Trudy Schaup, and Margaret Anton had a terrible fight about who was going to make the orange layer cake. Mona settled that by saying they could each make one; there was no such thing as too many orange layer cakes. Randy burned up a whole pan of cake-sale hermits, and put too much vinegar in the vinegar candy; Rush said it tasted like congealed French dressing. But on the whole things went well, and it promised to be a memorable fair. They relaxed their restrictions against adults in the case of Mr. Titus who pleaded to be allowed to make some marble cakes, and in the case of Mrs. Wheelwright, of Carthage, who was famous for her jelly doughnuts, and, of course, in the case of Mr. Cutmold, who was the auctioneer.

"Everything is going marvelously," sighed Mona, on Thursday.

But on Friday it rained. It rained all day. The children were no good in school. They kept staring out the windows, sighing gustily, and not hearing when their teachers called upon them.

Mona met Randy at recess. Her look of a tragedy queen was only slightly marred by the ink on her chin.

"We are ruined!" she said.

"Oh, listen, maybe it'll clear up before morning."

"No, it won't, we're ruined. Chris Cottrell says this is

probably the equinoctial storm, and that it's bound to last three days at least."

"Well, I won't believe it. Anyway, what is an equinoctial storm?"

"It comes at the times of year when days and nights are equal length; now, in September, and then again in March."

"Oh."

They listened to the rain in silence; then Randy said, "We can have the Fair indoors maybe."

"Yes, certainly, a splendid idea. We'll auction the cattle off in the living room, and the hogs in Father's study. Yes, that's a dandy idea!"

"Well, you don't have to be so mean about it, I was only trying to think of a way," said Randy, rather hurt.

"Okay, I know. But it's just more than I can bear to think of all those lovely boxes of penuche, and puffed-rice candy, and fudge, going to waste, to say nothing of the dozens of cakes, and the Chinese decorations!"

The bell rang then, and they went back to their classrooms with despair in their hearts. The cakemaking after school lost all its allure, but the girls went through it grimly. Every time a cake was in the oven, and therefore in the hands of destiny, the children rehearsed their parts in the show, and perfected their plans. But all the preparations which should have been joyously festive were gloom-tinged instead. The wet wind sighed strangely in the screens, and the rain drove harder than ever against the windows.

"You ought to hear it up in the cupola," Mark said. "It sounds like bullets."

"Oh, I hate it!" cried Mona, half in tears. "Horrible, vile, *pig* weather! Why couldn't it have held off?"

That night she lay in bed and listened to the roaring of the spruces. It's nothing to get so upset about, she tried to tell herself. What's an old fair, after all? It can be postponed. Think if it was Nazi bombers. Think if it was a storm in the South Pacific with only a tent over you. This isn't anything, it's less than anything at all. But, oh, I *wish* it would stop!

The world rocked like a cradle. After a while she fell asleep.

Why do I feel so blue? wondered Mona, when she woke up the next morning. My mind is full of something heavy and sad. What is it? Oh, the rain! She lay very still, listening. Holding her breath. She heard the loud, ruthless jeer of a bluejay; and then something else. A lawn mower! Mona's eyes flew open, and she saw the early-morning sunlight pouring through the windows.

"Oh, thank you!" cried Mona, leaping out of bed. "Thank you, thank you, thank you!"

It was a glorious morning, full of glorious work to do. Willy ambled about with a ladder, pinning up the decorations while Mona directed from below. Mark groomed the cattle, and helped Rush mow the lawn. Randy and Oliver sat among heaps of tissue paper, doing up presents for the grab bag. Children kept coming down the drive bringing their contributions of homemade cake, candy, popcorn balls, cookies. Daphne and Dave arrived earliest of all to set up the tents, and remained for the rest of the day helping with every sort of job. Hammers rang and saws sawed. Dogs barked, cows mooed, pigs squealed or rumbled, according to their size, and above all, shriller than all, were the high-pitched, intense voices of the children.

It was a marvelous day: September at its best. Hot in the sunshine, and cool in the shade, and the sky above was deep, deep azure like a gentian. Here and there, already, a tree had changed its color. There was a maple red as cardinal feathers, and back in the woods the hickories were turning yellow; but everything else was green.

Lunch was a dreamlike meal of sandwiches eaten out of doors, absentmindedly, with work still in progress. Cuffy would allow no one in the kitchen. She was making enough punch to slake the thirst of regiments.

At one o'clock Father arrived in the only Braxton taxi. It was wonderful to see him, they were all delighted, but their embraces were brief, their greetings briefer, and he was pressed into service before he had time to change his clothes. In no time at all he was standing on a kitchen chair tacking cheesecloth up on the summer house.

By two o'clock the transformation was complete. The Four-Story Mistake had become a fairground, and beautiful it was. The Chinese streamers were gorgeously looped from tree to tree, twined about trellises, and draped over branches. The jovial fish and dragons danced in the light September wind, and colored masks were strung in unexpected places. The Addisons' tents had been transformed from ordinary olive-drab backyard affairs to small Bedouin or Arabian shelters. Mona had done this by draping them with anything colorful and handy. A red tablecloth and a green hall rug for one. A yellow bedspread and Father's purple dressing gown, with the sleeves turned in (and not without a certain amount of resistance from Father) for the other. The result was that the tents were hot as Tophet inside, but wonderful to look at.

At two-thirty the people began to arrive. Oliver and a friend of his, Billy Anton, sold tickets at a point halfway up the drive. They had two chairs, a change box, a small table, a beach umbrella and four bottles of pop, and did a thriving business. People arrived in dozens. Farmers came for the sake of the auction, and their children came for the fun.

The Melendys and their friends had provided quite a lot of fun.

The Ten Cent Ride, for instance. Mark had thought that up himself. Most of the children who came to the Fair were farm children; the rest came from such small towns as Carthage and Eldred; a ride on the back of a tame, old mare was nothing new to them. But who had ever ridden on such a horse as this? For Lorna Doone had been decked out like a steed from King Arthur's stables.

Above her ears were bouquets of nasturtiums, her mane was braided with scarlet wool, and across her brow was a diadem of large glass beads. She wore a crimson saddle-cloth with fringed edges, and little bracelets of bells jingled above her hoofs (they were really only the old elastic garters sewn with bells that Mona and Randy had used for Morris dancing in their city school). . . . Lorna Doone was a horse of graceful temperament, she submitted serenely to all these trappings, and as Mark led her up and down the drive, and along the path through the woods, each small child upon her back felt that he rode as a king, and remembered long afterward that glittering and chiming journey.

The fortune-teller's booth was popular with people of all ages. The inside of the summer house was draped with blue cheesecloth left over from the show the Melendys had given in the winter, and pinned to it were stars and moons cut out of silver paper. There was a curtain across the door, and in the bluish gloom a table stood, on which were placed a round crystal paperweight, a candlestick, a rather sticky skull made out of plasticene, and a heavy book with an ornate binding which looked exactly like the book of a sorceress, but which once opened proved to be a compendium of the diseases of sheep. Still, nobody needed to know that.

Mona herself, after an inward struggle, had decided to sacrifice beauty for character, and was disguised as a very ugly, ancient soothsayer. She was wearing a wig of grey yarn, a costume which consisted of a long slip to which were pinned all the brightest scraps in Cuffy's piece bag, as many bracelets as she could collect, and a shawl over her head. Her face was crisscrossed with hand-made wrinkles applied with an eyebrow pencil.

She read one palm after another. The customers kept pouring in, and the dimes poured with them. Mona warmed to her work.

"You are going for a long trip across water," she might say, looking into the work-toughened palm of a farmer. "After the war's over, of course, and I *think* it's going to be Egypt. A trip up the Nile, maybe." Or, gazing wickedly at the hand of one of her schoolmates, she might say, "A man is about to enter your life. He is dark and handsome, even though his voice *is* changing. It looks like Harold Rauderbusch to me . . ."

The customers loved it. They giggled self-consciously and shifted their feet, but they hung on to every word.

Randy and Daphne presided at the cake booth. What a lavish display that was! At least at first; it did not last long. There were the three orange layer cakes, and the angel food cakes, the chocolate, mocha, sponge, raisin, and spice; the cupcakes topped with pink, white and chocolate; the trays of hermits, brownies, myriad cookies, and many another delicacy. And, dominating all, were the majestic marble cakes contributed by Mr. Titus. The girls worked like beavers, for the demands were heavy; Daphne was terrible at making change, and Randy was clumsy at tying packages, and from their efforts to keep the flies at bay some of the cakes tasted of Flit, but between them the girls managed pretty well, shortchanging only the minister and a lady from Braxton, and giving out only one really insecure parcel; though that, unfortunately, had contained a dozen of Mrs. Wheelwright's jelly doughnuts.

Punch was dispensed by Chris Cottrell in one of the Bedouin tents, and ice-cream cones by Trudy Schaup in the other. Even the two iron deer had been put to good use. Their antlers were twined with beads, paper streamers, and ribbons, and bound to the back of each were bulging saddlebags of brightly colored cloth. In front of the deer with the proudly raised head was a placard: "FOR BOYS! GRAB BAG! TEN CENTS A TURN!" And in front of the grazing deer was a similar proclamation for girls. The Melendys had worked hard over these gifts, and they were really good. In addition to the dime-store whistles, bubble pipes, puzzles, and bags of marbles, Oliver had contributed many of his small, precious, prewar metal planes and automobiles. Rush had surrendered a tiny, cherished flashlight, a harmonica, a pocketknife, and a cowboy belt set with colored stones. Randy had parted with two paintboxes, a set of crayons, and a white china pig. Mona's contribution consisted mainly of ten-cent jewelry: rings and large, flashing pins. She had also generously given four tiny bottles of perfume, and a box of incense.

No wonder the grab bags were such a success. Paper and string littered the lawn, eager fingers tore apart little bundles, and Pearl Cotton at the girls' deer and Jerome Hubbard at the boys' were already beginning to wonder if the supply would hold out.

This was not all. There still remained the boat ride and the Treasure Tree.

Steve Ladislas had lent the Melendys his little home-made, flat-bottomed boat, and Dave Addison took small passengers on a thrilling tour of the swimming pool. Half the children had never even seen a boat before; they hung over the side, and trailed their fingers and screamed at the sight of minnows; a whole ocean could not have pleased them more.

The Treasure Tree was really nothing but the tree house dressed up. Still, more than half the children had never seen a tree house before, and they were well-satisfied with it, even though there was no treasure on hand, unless you counted Rush, who was in charge.

The Fair belonged to the children, first of all. They had taken it over. In the background their mothers watched, gossiped with one another, and sat in the cool shade, babies on their knees. Their fathers, the farmers, gathered about the table, talked, spat, waited for the auction to begin.

"Jeepers, who are *those?*" cried Randy suddenly, during a lull in business.

Lumbering slowly through the crowd appeared two men. They walked as if it were difficult for them not to walk on all fours. They wore dark old denim clothes, more brown than blue by now, and on their heads were denim caps with long, sharp visors. All you could see of each one's face was eyes and nose: the rest was muffled in great waves of beard.

"Why, my goodness, they're the Delacey brothers," Daphne said. "They hardly ever come down out of the woods."

"Rush told me about them," Randy murmured. "I never really thought I'd see them."

"Hardly anybody ever sees them," said Daphne.

It was almost time for the auction. The cattle were all tied up outside the stable. The hogs were slumbering in one improvised pen; the melancholy Meeker poultry pecked and scratched in another.

At four o'clock Mr. Cutmold, the auctioneer, rang a large dinner bell. "Auction about to comm-ance!" he bellowed, in a voice that had been trained to volume. "Right over here, folks! Right over to the stable! Great opportunities for all!"

The crowd collected. Farmers to the front, of course, their faces grave: business was about to begin. Their wives came too, each with an identical pair of small children: one to carry, and one to hang on to. The other children deserted their pastimes at the sound of the bell, and joined the grown people. They pushed among the crowd, climbed bushes, and stood on railings. Rush came down out of his tree, Randy and Daphne left their cakes, the ancient gypsy stepped out of her booth with her wig on crooked, and Oliver and Billy Anton, prudently taking the money with them, deserted the box office on the principle that everybody who was coming must have come by now.

Mr. Cutmold was standing on an improvised auctioneer's block which was actually the kitchen table. He had a gavel in his hand, and an upended orange crate to knock on. Willy Sloper had been delegated to assist Mr. Cutmold, and he now led out the first cow.

"Here's a very fine little animal," boomed Mr. Cutmold. "A fine little first-calf heifer; a grade Holstein, two years old," and he proceeded to list her qualities and virtues. At the end he said. "What am I bid for this excellent creature?"

"Ten dollars," said a farmer instantly.

"Ten dollars!" shouted Mr. Cutmold, as if he had been stung by a bee. "*Ten dollars!* Give her away, why not? Do I hear fifteen?"

"Fifteen," said someone else.

"Kinda scrawny, ain't she?" murmured the first farmer's wife.

"I'll fatten her up. Twenty dollars!" said the farmer boldly.

"Do I hear twenty-five?" sang Mr. Cutmold alluringly, standing on the tips of his toes, and rolling his eyes.

He did hear twenty-five. Before the heifer was sold he heard eighty dollars.

"Eighty dollars!" said Oliver. "When I grow up I'm going to be a cow raiser."

"I'm going to be an auctioneer," said his friend Billy Anton, gazing raptly at Mr. Cutmold. "I got a good big voice for it already."

Willy led one of the older cows up to the auction block. She stood there staring dreamily at the crowd, her eyes like plums, and her jaws working with a slow, swiveling motion. Her tail flapped carelessly, arrogantly, at the September flies. She looked dignified and worthy of respect.

"Here we have a splendid animal," enthused Mr. Cutmold. "A four-year-old grade Holstein. An excellent milker, really excellent—"

"Thirty dollars," barked a large man.

"Thirty-five!" barked someone else.

"Forty!"

"Forty-five!"

And so it went. The proud creature was sold at last for a hundred dollars.

All the cattle brought handsome sums, and then it was the pigs' turn. One by one they were displayed: the gilts, the shoats, the cranky old sow and her litter of half-grown piglets. When the mean brown boar was brought out the Delacey brothers suddenly opened their shaggy mouths and growled in unison: "Ten dollars!"

Every time a bid was called the Delaceys instantly raised it with such fierce bear voices that they soon discouraged competition. The boar was theirs.

"The three of them should be very happy together," murmured Willy Sloper to Mr. Cutmold.

After the pigs were disposed of, Willy disappeared in the stable, a sudden heavy trampling was heard, and he came out leading the team.

These were good horses, though hard-worked. They stood there in the sunshine, quiet, broad-shouldered and strong. There was great patience and honesty about them. One could not look at them without a feeling of liking. Mark's throat felt hot when he saw them; he had known these horses for a long time. His fingers knew well the feeling of their coarse manes. He had fed them apples, harnessed them a thousand times, clambered onto their broad backs and ridden the pastures and woods for miles around, leaned his head against their sides and listened to the huge, tranquil rhythms of their hearts. He did not like to let them go.

"Now this team," cried Mr. Cutmold, a little hoarse by now. "This is a splendid team. A splendid team. Fine workers, strong, in prime condition. A mite thin, maybe, but that's soon remedied. Six years old, and come of good mixed stock. What am I bid?"

"One hundred dollars," stated a deep, melodious voice. Everyone turned. There on the fringes of the crowd stood a vastly fat man with a white round face like a Stilton cheese.

"That's Waldemar Crown," Rush whispered to Father. "He's the one that wrote the letter, the one who wanted Mark."

The faces that were turned toward the newcomer were staring and unfriendly. Even Mr. Cutmold's overworked jaw dropped open. He stood dumbfounded, with his gavel raised in mid-air before he caught himself up and went on . . .

"Ah, yes; ah, yes. This gentleman has bid one hundred dollars, do I hear one hundred and ten?"

"One hundred and ten," said a clear firm voice.

"Jeepers, it's Father!" hissed Randy.

"One twenty," said Waldemar Crown.

"One twenty-five," said Father.

The duel continued. Heads turned hypnotized from right to left: first to Father and then to Mr. Crown. Cuffy twisted her bead necklace so hard that she broke it and never even noticed. Randy thought this must be one of those times you read about, when you could hear a pin drop.

"Father looks mad," whispered Mona, in awe. "I never saw him look like that before."

Father stared straight ahead at Mr. Cutmold. There were unaccustomed spots of color on his cheeks, and his eyebrows were severely drawn together. Every time Waldemar Crown made a bid, he topped it.

"One-seventy," said Mr. Crown.

"One-eighty," retorted Father.

"Two hundred," snapped the fat man.

Father took a deep breath. A little vein stood out on his forehead.

"Two hundred and fifty!" he said.

Waldemar Crown hesitated and was lost. Mr. Cutmold leaped into the silence with alacrity.

"Two hundred and fifty do I hear two-fifty-five going going gone SOLD to the gentleman on my left: Mr. Martin Melendy of the Four-Story Mistake!"

People actually applauded, even the Delacey brothers. Mr. Crown slapped his broad-brimmed hat on his head and walked away, fat and furious.

"But gee, Mr. Melendy," Mark was protesting, "you shouldn't have done it! I *told* you you could have the team, just for a present, I mean. Gee, all that money, Mr. Melendy. I don't want to take it. Why did you ever do it?"

"Stop talking nonsense, Mark. I wanted to do it. Why, I couldn't let those good horses go to a blackhearted rapscallion like Crown, could I? I've heard tales of how he treats his animals. I'm glad to have that team."

"Father, you were wonderful!" Mona said. "You looked just like Humphrey Bogart."

"He made *me* think of Sydney Carton," Randy said.

After the drama of the horses, the chicken sale was

tame. The Melendys didn't even wait to see what became of the New Hampshire Reds (Rush said it sounded more like a football team than hens). But there were those among the crowd who had been living for this moment. The bidding was sharp and high.

The children vanished into the house to prepare for the show. The crowd thinned a little. Willy and Mr. Cutmold helped old Harrison Neeper load cows onto his truck, and crates of hens were placed clucking and complaining in ramshackle jalopies covered with back-roads dust.

"Now we've got a team, what are we going to do with it, Willy?" said Father.

"Say, Mr. Melendy, it sure raises up a lot of consequences. Can't let a team lay idle, you know. First thing, we'll have to start a real farm to work 'em on."

"Grain," said Father gloomily. "Oats and all that sort of thing. Plowed fields in the spring. That means a plow. Maybe I can borrow one. Then the mowing and shocking. That means a reaper or a combine. *Then* the threshing. That means— Oh, Lord," sighed Mr. Melendy, "what have I done?"

"Don't you worry, Mr. Melendy. I'll figure out a way to use 'em. And they'll make real nice company for Lorna Doone."

"Names," said Father. "Have they got names?"

"Jess and Damon. Damon is the one with the star on his forehead."

And now it was time for the show!

In the end they had decided to have it behind the house because the earth was more or less flat there, and the high clothesline was the logical place to hang the curtain. Benches and boxes were arranged to accommodate the audience, and the shed roof, cellar doors, and kitchen steps all made excellent vantage points.

Rush opened the show by dashing dramatically into the old Brahms Rhapsody. The piano had been moved outdoors, which didn't agree with it. It twanged like a cheap tin music box, but Rush did the best he could, and everybody was impressed. Next he played the Schumann Novelette he had been slaving over all summer.

After that Randy danced while he played. Yes, in her pink costume, and new pink ballet slippers, with a splendid disregard for grass stain, Randy danced like a fairy; floated above the mole hills and ambushed clothespins which would have tripped anyone less skillful. This was such a success that she had to improvise an encore.

After this Jerome Hubbard played "God Bless America," and "O Sole Mio" on his musical saw. Dave Addison recited the Gettysburg Address. Little Nancy Skeynes did her famous tapdance on an overturned washtub; Mark obliged by walking on his hands and turning handsprings, and then Mona, with the wrinkles scrubbed off her face, did a monologue which she had written herself. It was all about a captive French girl sending code messages to the British from an abandoned lighthouse, and was really by far the most successful thing about the show.

At the end everybody stood up and sang "The Star-Spangled Banner," with Rush playing a loud impassioned accompaniment, and the Fair was over.

"If only Mrs. Oliphant could have seen it," sighed Mona, "then it would really have been perfect."

Later, after the Red Cross money and Mark's livestock money had been counted (and fine substantial sums they were, too), the weary time of cleaning up arrived.

In the fading light the children moved about, taking down the Chinese decorations to be packed away for some future festival. Papers were littered all over the lawn. Mark was gathering them up in armfuls and stuffing them into a burlap sack, to be kept for the paper salvage. Rush took the Bedouin tents apart. In one of them he discovered Oliver, cross-legged on the ground, drinking left-over punch right out of the bucket.

"Oh, brother, are you going to be sick tonight!" said Rush with a sort of awe; a prophecy which subsequently proved correct.

Staggering with weariness they managed to clear away the worst of the mess, though plenty was left for tomorrow. Everybody helped: Cuffy, Willy, Father, everyone. Isaac and John Doe, let out of the house at last, hurled themselves about the lawn, leaping upon everyone and speaking with loud, expostulatory barks.

A plaintive mooing was heard in the distance. Rush looked wanly at Mark.

"Jeepers. The cows. We forgot to milk them!"

As they trudged toward the pasture Mark stooped and picked something out of the grass. It was one of Oliver's handmade tickets. Mark looked at it in the faint light, and smiled a little.

"'Admit one,'" he said aloud. "That's me, all right. I've been admitted. To a family. To a swell, real family. Boy, am I ever a lucky guy! No guy I ever heard of before was ever half so lucky!"

"Don't be a dope!" said Rush. "Who's lucky? Ran, and Mona, and Oliver, and I. We're the lucky ones. Didn't you know that?"

CHAPTER XV

Opus Three

It was the second of October. For weeks, now, Randy had been talking about having a picnic at the old, wrecked house in the woods. But one Saturday she and Oliver both had colds, and on the next it rained. Finally, however, the perfect day arrived.

Oliver, Mona, Randy, the dogs, and the lunch all went in the surrey. Oliver, with Mona beside him, was allowed to drive. It was a tremendous thing. He sat there quiet and intent, eyes straight ahead, brows frowning. You would have thought he was guiding a heavy cruiser through a fog.

Mark and Rush rode ahead; one on Jess, and one on Damon. They rode bareback, their legs dangling.

"It smells very fally," said Randy, closing her eyes and sniffing.

"'When yellow leaves, or none, or few, do hang,'" quoted Mona. "'Upon those boughs which shake against the cold,

"Bare ruin'd choirs where late the sweet birds sang.'"

"By William Shakespeare," added Oliver, with a loud sigh.

"See, even Oliver's on to you," giggled Randy. "But it's not cold, it's warm, and there are still lots of leaves on the boughs, though, of course, lots of them are falling, too."

They kept drifting down with that pensive, aimless flight which is like nothing else in the world. The sunshine seemed to come diminished through a faint film, though there wasn't a cloud anywhere.

It was the season of jays and crows. Their harsh voices pierced the silent air, and from everywhere in the woods came the hollow drilling of woodpeckers, and the dropping of acorns. Small creatures moved about the floor of the woods noisily. In the dry, crackling ocean of leaves the running squirrel sounded like a man, the hopping sparrow like a dog.

The children unharnessed Lorna Doone and put her with Jess and Damon into an open field to graze. The surrey stood, tall and narrow at the roadside; without a horse between its shafts it looked ridiculous and bereft.

Carrying baskets and hampers the children made their way through the woods, scuffling their feet joyfully in the dry leaves. Isaac and John Doe bounded and sniffed and pretended to be real hunting dogs.

At last they came to the remains of the old house. The tall chimney pointed like a finger at the sky. Among the fallen building stones ladies' tobacco had grown tall and flowered in aromatic, pearly bouquets. In the grass beneath the shabby apple trees small hard fruit lay scattered. One old skeleton tree, nothing but silver-grey wooden bones, lifted a single living branch to heaven, crowned with leaves and studded with little fire-red apples, like the pilgrim's staff.

The mourning dove's nest was an abandoned mound of sticks in the lilac bush. The swifts' nests in the chimney were empty, too. Presumably the woodchuck still occupied his tunneled apartment underground. No doubt he was sitting there now, still as a stone, listening to the footsteps overhead with irritation and foreboding.

Rush, Mark, and Randy pointed things out, explaining.

"What a marvelous place!" Mona cried. "Why didn't you ever bring me here before?" She loved all old things: old books, old legends, old wrecks of houses such as this.

"Look, that's the well over there," Randy said. "Let's go drop a stone in it. It makes a nice lonesome sound."

They pushed among scratchy blackberry canes and leaned over the side of the well.

"Why, look!" exclaimed Randy. "Something wonderful has happened!"

They peered down the mossy funnel, and there, a few feet below, looking up at them from a cranny between the stones was a clump of fringed gentians.

"Gosh, and they're hard to find," Mark said. "They're kind of rare around here."

"And the color of them," Randy said. "They must be the exact middle of the color of blue."

She almost forgot about dropping the stone. But Oliver didn't. He picked up a round pebble and held it out over the well. Then he let it fall. The sound it made when it met the water pleased him very much. He leaned down to search for another pebble.

Mona prowled about, exploring. She examined the building stones, looked up the chimney, and ate one of the little apples. She followed the leaves of lily of the valley far into the woods. What a garden to have, thought Mona, tame all spilled over into wild like this. That's what *I'd* like.

Pretend I live here, she thought. Pretend for some reason I'm all alone in the world and have no place to go. All I have is this chimney for a fireplace, and these stones, this well, this apple orchard. I build the stones into some kind of shelter, of course. I eat apples and nuts and berries and things. But what about winter? Oh, well, pretend there isn't any winter. Pretend it's the tropics.

Mona imagined wonderful dresses for herself all made out of mullein leaves stitched together; and jackets made of blue jay feathers, or woven of that very shiny golden kind of grass. All the wild things of the woods would be her friends: deer would eat from her hand, birds perch on her shoulder. A legend would grow up about her, people would speak of her as the Hermit Maid, or something like that. Very seldom would human eyes behold her, just now and then, when a hunter or trapper, or someone, caught a glimpse of her flitting through the forest, or running along the treetops like that girl in *Green Mansions*. They would bring tales back to their villages about her strangely haunting beauty, her solitary ways, her friendship with the woodland creatures.

Mona walked along with her eyes raised to the sky, a faint bemused smile on her lips. She was being the Hermit Maid with every fiber of her being.

A skyward gaze is all very well, but not unless you are walking on a fairly level surface. Mona's foot came into abrupt contact with one of the building stones and she suddenly fell flat on her face. She sat up for a moment, hugging her barked shin and stubbed toe, and rocking back and forth in pain and rage. Then with a deplorable but understandable impulse she stood up and gave the offending stone a furious shove with her foot.

The stone turned over on its side and disclosed a black rectangle of damp earth, frantic with centipedes. In the very center of this damp rectangle lay a blue glass bead, half buried.

The bead was large, about the size of a marble, and

made of a thick azure glass with bubbles in it. Mona picked it up, wiped it off with the palm of her hand. She couldn't believe her good fortune. The pain, forgotten, departed from her toe and shin.

"It's a sign," she murmured to herself. "It definitely is. Here it's been lying here all these years, maybe fifty or a hundred, and now I find it! I'll keep it for a lucky piece.

"Hey, look! Look, kids!" shouted the Hermit Maid, suddenly leaping like a she-goat over the stones and brambles. "Look what I found! I found a lucky piece!"

Oliver was still dropping pebbles into the well. He was lying on top of the round wall which encircled it, and he had a little pile of pebbles beside him. The autumn sun was warm upon his back, and a cool, deep breath came upward from the well. He would drop a stone; listen to its musical plop, and watch the dark circles spread away upon the water and dash in tiny waves against the wall. Each time he could see his reflection break to pieces, and then come together crazily, wavering and undulating, at first rapidly, then more and more slowly. When the reflection was quite still and whole again, he would drop the next pebble.

Finally he ran out of pebbles, but he was too lazy to climb down off the wall and look for more, and besides he was almost bored with the game. He stared down at the stone walls. They were richly furred with moss, and he could see little sprays of maidenhair fern sticking out of the cracks, and a cluster of brown, pointed toadstools. And the beautiful gentians, of course.

Oliver gazed at them covetously. They aren't so far down, he thought. I bet if I just leaned over—carefully, of course—way, w-a-a-y over—like this—and then *reached*—

And the next thing he knew he was wham-banging against the green walls, too fast to be hurt, and there was a noise somewhere like air squealing out of a balloon and then the ice-dark water closed over his head.

The squealing noise, of course, had been made by himself. The other children, building the fire, unpacking the baskets, had heard it with a sense of terror. Then had come the sound of an enormous splash. No one needed to be told what had happened. Instantly they were beside the well, looking over.

There, far below, they saw Oliver's round, wet head. He had just grabbed hold of a projecting stone, and was preparing to open his mouth and let go of a good howl when he looked up, face all crumpled, and saw them.

"Hello," said Oliver, quickly trying to straighten out his face.

The other children's voices came back to them.

"Oh, Oliver darling, are you sure you aren't dead?" cried Randy idiotically.

"Are you hurt?" "Isn't it cold?" "Can you hang on?" They all spoke at once.

Oliver said he didn't know if he was hurt or not, his

shoulder felt sort of blank. And, yes, it was cold, it was awful cold, and that he thought he could hold on for a little while.

"But what'll we do? How'll we ever get him out?" yelped Randy, jumping up and down. "We haven't any ropes or chains to pull him up with."

"*I* know," said Mona, suddenly inspired. "Mark, you can run quickest, you run down to the surrey and get Lorna Doone's reins! They ought to reach. And, Mark, wait, bring the blanket too!"

The rustle of Mark's flying feet could be heard for a long time. The dogs thought he was playing, and went bounding after him, barking blissfully.

"Are you okay, Fatso," inquired Rush, anxiously.

"Y-yes, I g-guesso," replied Oliver in a hollow voice, his teeth chattering. "Listen, Rush, do you think there's any sn-snakes down here?"

"You must be nuts!" said Rush heartily. "Of course there aren't. How do you think they'd get down and up? Fly?"

It seemed hours before Mark's returning rustlings were heard.

"I'm very cold, Mona," Oliver complained, beginning to cry at last. "I can't feel my feet even, and my fingers ache awful." The only warm thing he could feel was his own tears. Hot, they rolled down his cheek, and he caught each one on his tongue.

"Never mind, dearest. Just hold on a minute more. He'll be here right away. Honestly he will, darling," comforted Mona.

Randy was crying in sympathy and fear. She was never much good in a crisis, and this time all the mean things she had ever done to Oliver came back to her. The times she had said, "No, you can't come with us, you're too little." The times she had put things over on him, played tricks, laughed behind his back, because he was too young to know the difference.

"Don't you cry, Oliver," sobbed Randy. "When we get home I'm going to give you my whole box of pastels that Mrs. Oliphant gave me. And I'll let you use my best paintbox whenever it rains."

But Oliver, between crying and shivering, was past replying.

Luckily Mark came up gasping with the reins just then.

Unbuckled, they were long enough to reach Oliver. Mark and Rush and Mona hung far over the well, directing and encouraging.

"Loop the end around your middle, Oliver. Tie it good and tight, don't mind if it squeezes."

"I can't," came the hollow, reverberating wail from down the well. "My fingers won't work."

"They've *got* to work," shouted Rush. "You make 'em. You just make 'em!"

Randy couldn't bear to watch or listen. She held her

hands over her ears, shut her eyes, hopped on one foot. "*Get* him up! *Get* him up! *Get* him up!" she kept whispering under her breath.

And in the end, miraculously, with a great deal of yelping, sweating, hauling, and a lot of banging and scraping for Oliver, they did get him up. Dragged him onto the wall, blue with cold, teeth chattering, knees and knuckles bleeding.

"Mark and Rush, make a chair of your hands. Carry him down quick. We have to get him home right away."

But at this Oliver's mouth opened wide in grief. "The p-picnic!" he bawled. "I want to stay for the picnic!"

"Yes, and what about shock?" said Rush. "Keep the victim lying *down*, remember. Keep him warm, and all that. After all, who studied first aid?"

Mona had to admit that he was right.

There was a fire blazing in the old fireplace. They set Oliver down in front of it. They undressed him and wrapped him in their warm sweaters and the carriage blanket. They bound up his knees and scraped knuckles with handkerchiefs. They made much of him, and told him that he was a brave guy and a swell sport. After a while he stopped shivering, and by and by he began taking a personal interest in the hamburgers they were roasting over the fire. He sat up, watching hungrily, the blanket around his shoulders like an Indian brave's.

"I bet Billy Anton never fell down a well," said Oliver thoughtfully.

There were no further mishaps. In fact, it was a good picnic. The hamburgers and everything else tasted delicious. After lunch Mark and Mona went off exploring, Rush disappeared, and Randy sat beside Oliver and told him a story. Oliver's clothes fluttered about them everywhere. Pants hung from the lilac bush, jersey stretched taut on two sticks, socks and underwear draped over the blackberry canes. Every time Randy paused to draw breath, Oliver would say, "Go on." She was a little awed by the story herself, it came and came, like thread off a spool, and it was a wonderful story, all about an unknown volcano, near the North Pole, which was so warm that its sides were covered with flowering forests and warm streams, though it rose in the midst of a glacial waste of snow and ice. Marvelous people lived on this mountain: blond, strong, beautiful. Randy had a good time giving them names: Queen Tataspan, King Tagador, and Tatsinda, the heroine. Maybe I better be a writer too, thought Randy, as she told the story. A ballet dancer, an artist, and a writer. I'd like to be a fancy skater too, if I could ever learn how.

"Also Tatsinda was a wonderful ice skater," she said aloud. "She used to go skating on the Arctic Ocean, on skates made of pure gold. The volcano had veins of gold and silver in it too, you know . . ."

She turned and looked at Oliver. He was suddenly fast asleep. Randy sighed. She remembered that she had promised, in an unguarded moment, to give him her wonderful box of pastels. But here he was, safe and sound, full of hamburger and fast asleep, was it really, really necessary? She looked down at her brother again, with his still-damp hair, the dried-milk mustache on his upper lip, the bound-up hands resting pathetically on his chest. Yes, yes, it was necessary, Randy knew. Oliver was worth all the pastels in the world, and all the paintboxes too.

She got up and stretched and wondered where everyone had gone. She wandered along the ridge and suddenly came upon Rush sitting bolt upright on a stump with a very strange expression on his face.

"Why, what's the *matter*? Are you sick? You did eat an awful lot," said Randy.

"Please shut up, would you?" said Rush beseechingly. "I'm thinking."

"For heaven's sake. Why? What about?"

"Opus Three," Rush said.

"You mean you're composing?"

"Yes. Please shut up."

"All right. Only I bet Mozart never looked as if he was going to throw up when he was composing."

Randy started to go away.

"Wait a minute, Ran. Have you a piece of paper? I've got a pencil, but no paper. And I'm scared I might forget this."

"Would a paper napkin do? I'll get you one."

"Sure, anything." Rush sat there waiting and listening to the music in his mind. It was really beginning to come, and this time, by gum, it really looked as if it might be good. He must seize each little note by the tail as it went flying by. He must catch it, and he would catch it!

At four o'clock it was already cool, and they were on their way home.

Rush drove the surrey this time, and Randy rode home on Jess.

Oliver in his newly dried clothes curled up against Mona.

"Do you think Cuffy will be mad when she hears how I fell down the well? I bet she will, don't you? Don't you, Mona?"

"No, silly. If she is it won't be at you. And I don't think she'll be mad anyway. I think she'll be thankful to have you safe."

"It was smart of you to think of the reins, Mona," said Rush, from the front seat. "I don't know what we would have done . . ." He felt fond of her, and of his family. In fact he loved the whole world. He had Opus Three snared on a paper napkin in his pocket, and Lorna Doone was taking him home to his piano as fast as she knew how. He could hardly wait to hear how those notes would really sound.

Randy and Mark were the first ones home, though. Jess and Damon had had a lazy day, and now they took the road at a heavy, work-horse gallop. Randy's teeth shook in their sockets, sparks flew in front of her eyes, and she knew, beyond doubt, that it was going to hurt her to sit down for several days. She admitted none of this to Mark, but she was relieved and happy when they turned in at the gate of the Four-Story Mistake.

"Home again," said Randy, as they rounded the bend and came down the slope. She said it as casually as if she had said, "It's a nice day."

"Home again," echoed Mark. But he felt as though it would be a long time before he was used to those words. Home . . . Well, that's quite a word in itself if you're not used to it, but to have it followed by *again*! . . . It was a phrase he was to use hundreds of times from now on. But today it was still new.

"Home again," repeated Mark. And he said it as solemnly and joyfully as if he had said the word "Amen;" and quickly followed it with the word "Hooray!"

About the Author

Elizabeth Enright (1909–1968) was born in Oak Park, Illinois, but spent most of her life in or around New York City. Originally envisioning a career solely in illustration, she studied art in Paris, France, and at the Parsons School of Design in Manhattan. In 1937, her first book was published, quickly proving her talent for writing as well as for drawing.

Throughout her life, Elizabeth Enright wrote and illustrated numerous award-winning children's books. Among those awards were the 1939 John Newbery Medal for *Thimble Summer* and a 1958 Newbery Honor for *Gone-Away Lake*. The first of the Melendy Quartet, *The Saturdays*, was published in 1941. It was followed by *The Four-Story Mistake*, *Then There Were Five*, and *Spiderweb for Two: A Melendy Maze*. Ms. Enright was also a highly regarded writer of short stories published in magazines, such as the *New Yorker* and *Harper's*. Her stories are assembled in four collections: *A Moment Before the Rain*, *Borrowed Summer*, *The Riddle of the Fly*, and *Doublefields*. Translated into numerous languages throughout the world, Ms. Enright's writings have been loved by many generations, and they continue to find an audience with young and old alike.